After Dark

by Michael A. DiBaggio

With Illustrations by

Shell "Presto" DiBaggio

Book Cover Painted by

Matty Lasuire
http://americandork.daportfolio.com

Part of the Ascension Epoch
http://www.ascensionepoch.cc

Acknowledgments

The author would like to thank the following:

• **Benjamin Feehan, Theodore Minick, Richard Rohlin, and Russell Williams** - For beta reading, constructive criticism, and support for this project.

• **Blambot.com** - For the fonts used on the cover

• **Christos Karapanos** - For the Photoshop rain brushes used on the cover (https://www.facebook.com/pages/Christos-Karapanos-Art/168866523208953)

Contents

Tough Gig

My name is Sebastian Pereira, and ever since I can remember, I wanted to be a superhero.

When I was five, I was at the bank with my aunt when a couple of creeps robbed the place. She tried to cover my eyes as the Target beat the hell out of them, but I saw it all, and I never forgot it.

At first, everyone thought it was cute when I'd tell them I was going to be a vigilante when I grew up. But when I kept saying that into my teens, people started to get worried. My priest mocked me, and the preceptors told me I was being silly. My parents wagged their fingers, their voices full of disapproval: "Sebastian, they're are as bad as the crooks they go after! Don't you know how often they get killed?"

But they were all hypocrites. I heard them gush about the Sentinel. I noticed that look of envy whenever they saw someone zipping across the sky under their own power. I remembered how Aunt Carol got all weak-kneed and doe-eyed when the Target winked at her. And I went on imagining beating up bank robbers or pulling kittens out of trees and babies out of burning buildings like The Flame and Web Wonder did (before he became a monster, anyway).

But I knew they were right about one thing: it was a tough gig to get into without special powers, and I was no talent. Nobody in my family was, so far as anyone would tell me. Sure, there were lots of non-talent vigilantes, and famous mystery men who worked for the patrol services, but doing it that way was even harder, almost equivalent to getting a pro sports contract. So eventually I faced reality and started thinking about what I could really do – but I never totally put it out of my mind.

Then when I was 15, puberty gave me something besides acne and a fear of tight shorts.

A woman at the train station left her notebook on the bench next to me. I tried to return it to her, but when I picked it up, I started to see and hear and even smell things that I knew weren't coming from anywhere in the station. Disconnected memories of thoughts I'd never had buzzed around my skull. It was like living in stereo, one part of me in the terminal, another part of me hitching a ride inside this lady's brain.

I dropped the notebook back on the bench and those memories went away; when I picked it up again, they came back.

Psychometry is telepathy's homely sister that nobody ever asks to the dance. Instead of reading other people's minds, you pick up the psychic residue they leave on other objects, which usually isn't anything at all unless its associated with something really traumatic (like a murder weapon) or impressed on it by the sheer psychic weight of lots of people (like a public bathroom — *yick*). The former can be overwhelming while the latter is just a big non-linear jumble of sights and feelings you can't make sense of.

Yeah. I wanted to roll two 10-sided dice and pick a new power from the list, but it doesn't work that way.

Even worse, my psychometry was pretty low grade (Talent Level 3, speaking clinically), so I was

only able to consistently pick up the really strong signals and the rest was a crap shoot. The cute lab tech at Pitt's Reich Center said this was a blessing. She told me about some big-time sensitives she'd met who had to wear gloves all the time, and a particularly bad case, shrouded in a perpetual bubble of psychic white noise, who wouldn't communicate with his family anymore.

It wasn't much comfort. I can't tell you how aggravating it was to think that I'd won the talent lottery only to manifest a lame power. I was a dud, a spoon-bender, unable even to provoke real curiosity. I was that loser at the bar who tried to impress chicks by wiggling his ears or telling them he's only 6 years old because he was born on February 29th.

For a while, the limit of my ambitions were to fondle towels from the girls' locker room or contact-snooping on strangers at restaurants. But then I got tired of the cheap voyeurism and attempts to live vicariously through utterly boring people. I said to myself: "You know what? Most people don't even get psychometry. Why not use the gift? Why not be a superhero after all?"

I went back to lifting and started running. I read biographies of the greats. Body and mind were harnessed for my true purpose.

But then I started to doubt myself. What if everyone was right? What if I got killed? Was I completely crazy?

**

It was the second week of February and pitchers and catchers were reporting to Spring Training down in sunny Texas and Florida. Back in the 'Burgh, on the other hand, it was still cold as Hell if Hell got cold, so our first practices were indoors. In a corner of the St. Bonaventure gymnasium, two of my friends and I played pepper to shake out the cobwebs.

The baseball, a survivor from last year and now more a brownish yellow than white, skipped erratically off the laminated hardwood and flew toward my hip at an awkward angle. I shifted down and swept the glove across my body, snatching the ball with a leathery pop, then side-lobbed the ball back toward the batter.

Alex Shepherd's forearms, thick as a knotted rope, rippled with every compact swing as he drove the ball back at us. Alex was taller than me and more athletic but not as good-looking; he had had his nose broken one time too many in boxing matches.

"Take it – yow! – easy!" Ben, Alex's younger brother, grimaced as the ball rocketed off his hip. He rubbed the tender spot and shot a dirty look over his shoulder as he trotted off to get the ball.

"Yeah man, we're only twenty feet away," I said. "Haven't you ever played pepper before?"

"We tried once," Alex answered, slanting the aluminum bat over his shoulder. "Then the groundskeeper yelled at us, 'Can't you delinquents read?' he said. There was this big 'No Pepper' sign painted on the wall."

"If pepper is outlawed, only outlaws will play pepper." I took a minute to wipe away the hair plastered to my sweaty forehead and then told them, apropos of nothing, "I've decided to become a vigilante."

The Shepherd brothers looked at me blankly, the tangential remark seeming to have disabled conscious thought.

I needed a reality check from people I could trust. Alex had been my best friend for years, and Ben was solid enough. At least they weren't automatic scoffers like everyone else, so if they really thought it was a stupid idea, I'd drop it and forget about it once and for all.

I nodded thoughtfully and added, with a practiced nonchalance, "What do you think about the name Doom Specter?"

Alex and Ben looked at each other, then smiled.

"Sweet idea!" Ben exclaimed.

Alex high-fived me. "Yeah, man, good name."

I knew they'd understand.

***

That very night, I donned my first crude costume: an old hooded sweatshirt, rip-stop pants, and a wool ski mask that was far too hot for the weather and made my nose itch. I left my house by my bedroom window – not because I had to, but because it was more dramatic. I had a can of pepper spray and my pop's old brass knuckles for punishing thugs, and a bundle of zip ties to tie them up when I finished. I didn't have a clue what I was doing, but that night I couldn't care less. Somewhere out on those dark streets lurked thieves and murderers, arsonists and rapists, and tonight they were prey for the Doom Specter.

Well, the prey were pretty safe, whereever they were.

I had the vague idea that walking a beat around my neighborhood would be enough, and if not, then psychometry would fill in the gaps. It was a laughably stupid idea. I couldn't remember the last time anyone had so much as keyed a car on my block.

So I tuned into the police scanners with my mobi, and sure enough started to hear about burglaries and shootings – usually on the other side of the city.

So the next weekend, I patrolled on my bike and wore down both my legs and the electric motor trying to react to distant reports of crime. If I was lucky, I'd arrive just in time to see one of the Troubleshooter wagons drive off. A couple times, even the worthless city cops beat me to the scene. Talk about humiliation.

Once, there was a fire call only twelve blocks away. It was late and I'd already run down the battery, but I pedaled furiously, uphill the whole way. I was three blocks away, panting and sweating, when the fire trucks passed me.

It was discouraging, but I wasn't defeated. I thought that if Doom Specter couldn't save the day, maybe he could solve a few mysteries. Disappearances, impossible robberies, cases the patrol companies and private detectives had given up on. I could be the next Sherlock Holmes or, more appropriately, the next Carnacki.

Unfortunately, a lot of people were strangely reticent about talking to a guy in a ski mask. Added to that, my ESP was unreliable. The psychic detective angle wasn't panning out either.

Three weeks into it, I was really frustrated. I was spoiling for a fight and so I found one: three punks

spraying graffiti onto the walls of an old glass factory. Now, this building was a burned-out husk, and in retrospect a few more dirty limericks and flaming penises might have even improved the look of the place, but I tell you right then I just didn't care. I threaded my fingers through the brass knuckles and leaped out of the bush, screaming at the top of my lungs: "Run for your lives, scumbags!"

I went right for the biggest one, throwing hands and feet, knees and elbows. Glass broke, bricks flew, blood sprayed.

There were three of them and only one of me, and my psychometry sure as hell wasn't going to even the score…

But something else did.

***

I didn't recognize the face whose glassy eyes, half-occulted behind puffy and purple sockets, stared through me. I blinked twice and reached fumblingly for the light switch, already squinting in anticipation of the bright glare of the lightbulbs.

The light rinsed away the violet shadows that made the face seem so much older, more hollow, and pale than the one I expected to see. I saw the familiar soft inflection point of my cheek beneath the ragged laceration that ran from below my left eye to the hinge of my jaw, and I could see that the profoundly arching frown really was my mouth beneath the lumpy abrasions and dried brown blood that camouflaged it. My distant stare sharpened at this recognition of my own battered face in the bathroom mirror, and at once the pain sharpened along with it.

My sweaty hands clamped around the edge of the sink as my head slumped queasily forward. Strings of bloody saliva, dark and syrupy, trickled off my lips.

I probed the tender interior of my mouth with my tongue, testing whether any of my teeth were loose, carefully avoiding the bloody hole that my rattling molars had torn inside my cheek. I'd already done this at least five times since I pulled myself off the pavement, using the same aluminum pipe one of the vandals beat me with as a crutch. Finally satisfied that an emergency trip to the dentist needn't be added to my list of concerns, I turned on the faucet and let the cascade of cold water wash over the nape of my neck.

"Jesus, you're leaking blood on the towels! If my mom were here, she'd flip out." Alex said.

I felt guilty about using his bathroom as a dispensary, but his house was a half mile closer than mine, and I wasn't entirely confident I'd make it all the way back home on my own. Plus, there was the dimly remembered fact that his parents were gone somewhere, a second honeymoon in Cuba or something. With my father's insomnia, not to mention my sister's nosiness, I would've had almost no chance of cleaning myself up without being noticed at my own house.

"Swallow a couple of these when you're done," Alex said, rattling a small bottle of Ibuprofen next to my ear. When I didn't answer, he manually curled my fingers around the bottle.

"You can still see straight, can't you? Does anything feel broken?" he asked, tearing open a bag of cotton balls to wet with hydrogen peroxide.

I turned my head toward him in answer to the first question, and then grimaced in pain as the streaming water found a paper-thin cut in my scalp that I hadn't noticed before.

"Knee's worse than anything," I said. "Landed on it when I fell."

"I have ice packs you can take with you. What's that stuff all over your pants?"

"Paint." I lifted my head out of the water and looked myself over again. 'You're going to need a lot of ice,' I thought, remembering that this was how my sister Olivia looked after getting stung by a wasp, right before her eyes swelled completely shut.

"Paint?" Alex's eyebrows went up. "They threw paint on you?"

I shook my head, which knocked off my equilibrium and set my vision spinning. I had to grab hold of the sink to steady myself again. Alex grabbed my shoulder and urged me to sit down before I fell over and spilled the rest of my skull all over his parents' newly remodeled bathroom.

"No. It was me," I told him as I slumped down onto the toilet. "I blew up their spray cans – one of them in his hands. I blew them up…with my mind. Just by thinking about it. They ran like hell!"

I massaged my split knuckles as I reminisced. "It was something else, man. A real spectacle."

"Yow, that's an ugly cut. It might need stitching," Alex remarked. He must have thought I was delirious.

I sat quiet for a moment and just smiled. "I think," my voice quavered with excitement, "I think I have a real talent now."

"I think you've been hit in the head and you're babbling."

"Oh yeah?" I cocked my head toward the running faucet and the water stopped.

"Holy shit," Alex muttered. "Did you do that?"

My smile bloomed into an exuberant, bloody-toothed grin. I let the water flow again.

I'd gotten to roll the dice again, and this time I picked a winner. "Next time, it'll be different," I said.

"Next time?"

You might have looked at me and said, "Listen buddy, you just got your ass handed to you over something really stupid", and you'd be right. But that was irrelevant. I was on the right track; the big man upstairs was looking out for me, rooting for me. I just needed a little more: more resources, more gear, more preparation. Most of all I needed reinforcements.

"Yeah. Next time," I said. "I could use someone to watch my back, though."

Alex thought it over. "Yeah. Sure, why not?"

"Really?"

"I've actually been thinking about it for a while. Besides, you obviously need somebody who can fight. I even thought of a killer name: The Mysterious X!"

I blinked. "Why?"

"What do you mean?"

"Why do you think that's a good name?"

"What's wrong with it?"

"Nevermind. But now that you mention it, I think it's time I retired Doom Spectre. It never felt quite right, and now I have a talent that suggests some good names–"

15

"Water Wizard," Alex offered.

I snorted. "You're terrible at this."

"Well, then what?"

"Torrent."

First Impressions

Balanced on the tips of her toes, Evangeline reached for a thin volume on the top shelf and then stopped, letting her pink-nailed fingertips drag down the spine of the aged text, softly scratching on the embossed golden letters that called her attention. She frowned, suddenly unsure of why she should care about Sumatra's giant rats, and started to feel guilty about wasting tuition money on whimsy. The St. Bonaventure Academy and its paradigm of completely self-directed education had seemed like a dream come true when she begged her father to send her there, but now its vast, open libraries and its sophisticated labs and workshops seemed like a paralyzing over-abundance of opportunity.

She stared at the face of her slender silver wristwatch as it ticked on toward 2:30 and the end of a day in which she had done absolutely nothing. This deadline would come and go without anyone noticing except herself, but it felt as stressful as the five minute warning on a final exam. She let out an anxious, almost whimpering sigh and wished that one of the instructors, instead of waiting to be engaged, would take pity on her and assign a bundle of homework.

'I really don't have the discipline or the motivation to make it here,' she thought, and not for the first time today.

"Hey, new girl."

Evangeline turned toward the voice, only a little apprehensively, and flashed a nervous smile at the three teenage girls standing at the end of the aisle. Arranged in increasing height from left to right, they resembled a flight of steps with sardonic faces. The shortest (about as tall as Eva) was a peroxide blonde wearing gaudy plastic earrings the size and color of clementines that stretched her earlobes. She wore her hair in a severely tight ponytail and her thin, high-arched eyebrows, plucked to the point of surrender, left her looking permanently surprised. The biggest was a giant brunette, seemingly half as wide as she was tall, with small circles for eyes set deep behind her flabby cheeks. But the girl in the middle was stunning. She had dark eyes and a flawless, olive-colored complexion – a truly beautiful face that not even the disdainful sneer on her lips could diminish – and her black hair was lustrous and bouncy to a degree Evangeline could only attain in her dreams. But the worst of it was that she had the kind of curves that even a Catholic school dress code couldn't hide. Eva, who had never before felt really insecure over her own figure, suddenly felt frumpy and boyish by comparison.

"Hi," Evangeline squeaked over the lump in her throat. It was easy to guess what was coming.

"We like your blouse. Where'd you get it?" the little blonde asked. She had a hard time keeping a straight face.

Evangeline automatically examined her simple, seashell-colored garment, smoothing out one of the pleats that bisected an ornamental breast pocket. "I don't remember. I've had it for a while." She nervously brushed back a scarlet ringlet that hovered over the corner of her eye and held her breath in anticipation of the forthcoming insult.

"I have one just like it," the blonde said, and she and the tall, fat one snorted simultaneously. "Except mine didn't come covered in cat hair."

Evangeline winced. She regretted pestering Marshmallow all morning. She had been too nervous about her first day at school to sleep late or eat breakfast and the fat Ragdoll cat provided the needed distraction.

'Just don't make eye contact and you can walk past them, Eva,' she told herself and steeled her nerves to leave.

The blonde continued to taunt her. "I love fur, it's so stylish!"

"Whatever," Evangeline muttered, her volume almost too low to hear. She turned her back on them and started walking toward the opposite end of the aisle.

"Gawd, look at that skirt!" The fat one took a break from her affected snickering to reveal her incongruously nasal voice. "It does look like her mom dresses her!"

The blonde hurried to ¯agree. "Totally, Laura. And with her old clothes!"

Evangeline turned quickly, fixing them in a furious glare. "My mom doesn't live with me, you cow!" she snapped, her voice shaking. The three vipers were silent for a moment, the blonde's penciled-in eyebrows peaking weirdly at her temerity. Suddenly the black-haired one started laughing and, after a few seconds, the blonde joined in, exchanging condescending looks with one another. The fat girl's

already red cheeks went a deeper crimson, obviously stung by the cow remark and suspicious that her companions were actually laughing at her. Evangeline knew better.

'Why did I say that?' she thought. But she knew why. Part of it was that she hoped, futilely, that they might feel ashamed with themselves for picking on her if only they felt bad for her.

'God, that's so pathetic,' Evangeline chastised herself, her pale, freckled cheeks turning red with shame.

"Aww! No wonder," the blonde interjected with a mock frown. "Did mommy dump you in the alleyway?"

"That's not it, Angie," the gorgeous raven-haired girl, obviously their leader, spoke for the first time. "She's telling us her daddy dresses her. And undresses her. Touches her in her secret places." Her two sycophants laughed triumphantly at the perverse remark. Evangeline froze and stared at her with a horrified expression on her face. The girl's cruel, thin lips curled at the corner with real delight.

Evangeline felt like a perfect spineless buffoon just standing there, but she lacked the energy to do anything else. She felt violently ill, aware now that a new figure had appeared behind them, doubtless come to share in the revelry.

"Leave her alone, Vanessa," a stern male voice demanded.

All four of the girls looked at the interloper in surprise. Evangeline thought he was vaguely familiar, but in the way of looking interchangeable with the other boys here: dark brown hair, blue eyes, wire-framed glasses, and only little taller than the chieftain of the mean girls.

Angie clucked her tongue and Vanessa barked: "Why don't you mind your own business, loser?"

"Why don't you take your own advice?" returned Evangeline's champion. He looked taller now as his shoulders squared and his chest filled with air. "Christ Almighty! Accusing her dad of molesting her? Really? That's low even for you witches. Now out of the way, Meat Curtains!" He shouldered Laura to one side and waved Evangeline through.

"Don't shove me, faggot!" growled the fat brunette, throwing her thick arms into his back.

The boy's face darkened and his right arm, which had been hanging loosely at his side, cocked back. Laura must have thought he was really going to punch her because she immediately jerked backwards and her chubby eyelids reeled back in fear.

Evangeline sprinted to the doorway with her head down. If she didn't look up, she wouldn't have to lie about not seeing him deck Laura. She quickly ran down the first flight of steps and then waited tensely, but there were no screams nor the fist-on-raw-meat crack she'd learned to expect from watching movies. Instead, the young man calmly followed her through the doorway.

His eyes met hers and, as they lingered, his lips curved into the most crooked, self-satisfied smirk she'd ever seen. She felt her body temperature flare, knew her cheeks were reddening again, and lowered her gaze so quickly that her hair bounced down from her shoulders and fell in a crimson curtain over her eyes.

22

Eva bit her lip and pressed back against the wall, rigid with shyness, waiting for him to say something or walk by or do anything at all to break the awkward tension. All she heard (for she couldn't – wouldn't – look at him) was a jingling of metal and the door re-open. Cautiously, she brushed back her hair and looked toward him out of the corner of her eye. He had turned his back, dug a coin out of his pocket, and lobbed it back into the library. "Here's a quarter," he said to the girls, "buy yourselves a personality."

The remark caught her by surprise and she nearly choked trying to quiet her laughter. Evangeline pushed her hair all the way back now and looked at her rescuer with fascination as he descended the stairs toward her. Whether it was a change in the lighting or a change in her mental perspective she didn't know, but the young man had suddenly become handsome. She was captivated by his swagger and the defiant way he angled his chin. There was an intensity in those intelligent eyes and a manly strength in the horizontal plane of his shoulders that belied the softness implied by his delicate eyeglasses and still-boyish face. It hardly seemed possible to Evangeline that she could ever have found him interchangeable.

She waited for him to say something, but he didn't. Instead he pushed open the door and held it for her.

"Thank you," she broke the ice, unconsciously brushing her black skirt for clinging cat hair. "For sticking up for me, I mean. And holding the door. You didn't have to."

"Sure I did," he said, "And you're welcome."

"That line with the quarter was great! I wish I could have thought of that!" She cocked her head sideways, squinting up at him as she ducked under his arm and stepped out into the corridor.

He gave a wan half-smile, flicking his eyes down at her for a second, then sighed. "I'm going to catch hell for that tomorrow. I wish it was socially acceptable to knock a broad's teeth out of her mouth," he announced. "They're twats. Don't pay attention to them."

Evangeline smiled at his easy way with vulgar insults. She had always been told that nice boys didn't talk like that.

"I won't," she said. It was a lie, of course. It was easy enough to say you won't be bothered by something like that, and quite another to actually manage it.

"Easier said than done, I know," he replied in a moment of psychic rapport. "But those girls are a minority. There are lots of friendly, decent kids here though."

"Like you?"

He shrugged, then smiled. "Nicer."

"I'm Evangeline," she introduced herself, proffered her hand in awkward greeting. "Do you live nearby?"

He shook her hand uncomfortably, nodded. "Yeah, I do. Oh, I'm Sebastian. I'm about ten blocks away, in Shadyside."

"Me too! I just moved here last week, we're renting a house on Summerlea Street."

Sebastian answered without stopping. "I live closer to Chatham. You know where that is?"

"The girls' college? Yeah, I think so," Evangeline confirmed. She lengthened her stride to keep up with his quick pace.

Sebastian stopped abruptly and she almost tripped over her own feet while trying to adjust. He cocked his head when he looked at her, appearing a little bashful, and his tone was tentative. "Do you want me to walk you home, Evangeline? Or is somebody coming to-"

"Oh, sure!" she exclaimed, then, thinking she was acting a bit too excited, dialed it back. "I would like that. I... don't fully know my way around, yet."

"Cool," he said, nodding. "Are you almost ready to go then? I just have to go to my locker quick."

"Yeah, me too."

"Meet you at the side exit then?" Sebastian suggested, pointing down the hall toward a pair of giant doors with brass latches that reminded Evangeline of the doors behind a castle's drawbridge.

"I'll be there in a jiffy," she said and trotted down the hall towards the girls' lockers.

Evangeline had to contend with a crowd of teenage girls gossiping and idly milling around the tight locker spaces, so that by the time she'd retrieved her jacket and got to the door, Sebastian was already standing there waiting.

"I thought you might have left without me," he said, turning and hauling on the heavy door with both hands until it opened onto the campus. A stiff, deliciously cold wind filled the corridor and whipped Eva's hair back in tangled strands.

"Sorry. You know how girls are." She squinted at the bright sunlight and looked around, trying to orientate herself.

"This way," Sebastian said with a cock of his head. "Hey, that jacket looks a little light for this weather. Do you want mine? Here, you can borrow my gloves..." He was already pulling them off his hands when she emphatically declined.

"No, no, no! I'm fine. I'm really warm, actually. I'm...always really warm."

"Ah, OK," he said. "I just thought the Pittsburgh weather might have caught you by surprise. It was pretty warm last week, but the weather changes quickly in this town. It's false spring. Where did you move from?"

"Most recently from Kansas, but my dad and I've lived all over," she answered.

"Oh, wow. From out of the country, then. I thought you might have moved from another part of Pennsylvania or Kanawha or something."

"Nope. I was actually born in the 'Planes. This is my first time in the Commonwealths." She peeked up at him. "What about you?"

"Born here," Sebastian replied. "I've gone to a couple of places before, but nowhere so far away as Heartland. Do you move a lot, then? Is it for your dad's job?"

"Yeah. He's a mining engineer."

"That's interesting."

Evangeline shrugged. "He says he follows the money, but I think he just doesn't like to stay in one place too long."

"Oh. Do you think you'll be staying in Pittsburgh for long?" Sebastian asked.

"He's on a one year contract. We'll see, I guess. I'd like to stay here until I go off to college."

They paused at a street corner as a line of cars zipped by. "If you turn over there, you can shortcut around the traffic," Sebastian said, angling his head in the direction they were walking while he kept his hands in his pockets. Evangeline noticed him shivering and briefly considered doing likewise.

'No, don't start doing that again,' she scolded herself. 'You don't need to broadcast it, but don't lie about it.'

"So what do you think of the 'Burgh so far?" Sebastian broke in as they hurried across the street.

"I like it! The scenery is a nice break from Kansas. Everything is so flat out there. And it looks like there's more to do here."

"Yeah, there's some cool stuff going on in the city and nearby," he allowed. "It's not Meridian Harbor or anything, but it's not totally boring."

"Maybe you can show me them sometime?" Evangeline ventured.

Sebastian smiled and looked straight ahead. "I'd be happy to," he said in a quiet voice. Neither of them said anything for nearly half a block. Finally, clearing his throat, he said: "Don't take this the wrong way, but…Evangeline. I like that. That's a beautiful name."

Evangeline looked down at her feet bashfully and chuckled. "Why would I take that the wrong way?"

He snorted with embarrassed laughter, held out his hands. "I have no idea."

28

"Thank you, Sebastian." She looked up at him as they walked; he glanced over at her, but then quickly looked away.

"Are you named after the Longfellow poem?" he asked, running his gloved hands through his short hair.

"You know that poem?" Evangeline was beaming. "Are you a Longfellow fan?"

Her ardor surprised him, and he laughed a little. "A fan? Well, I don't know about that, but I do know the poem. And I appreciate good literature."

"Oh, that's exciting! I don't think I've ever talked to anyone my own age who knew 'Evangeline'," she gushed. "I love poetry, especially the Romantics, but I'm fond of the early American stuff too. Who's your favorite poet?"

"Ashbless."

"Ashbless?! You're kidding!" Evangeline replied, so carried away by this unexpected new dimension of her companion that she forgot to politely mask her distaste. "That's...obscure. Well, who's your favorite author?"

"The Marquis de Sade," declared Sebastian without a moment's hesitation.

Evangeline's brow began to furrow in concern. "Uhm...do you like Shakespeare?"

"I love *Titus Andronicus*," he said.

The declaration seemed to have the weight of physical force. Evangeline stopped walking; she felt lightheaded.

Sebastian smiled at her. "I am kidding, yeah."

Evangeline gave a profound frown. "You have a weird sense of humor, Sebastian."

"Ha! And just ten minutes ago you were telling me how much you appreciated my wit."

"You were using your powers for good then," she smirked.

"Never! I only use my powers for awesome," he riposted, and they both laughed.

"Is that your superpower? Being able to come up with the perfect witty rejoinder right on time?" Evangeline said.

Sebastian raised his eyebrow minutely, but said nothing.

"You know the French call that 'the wisdom of the staircase,'" said Evangeline.

"I did use it on the staircase," he said.

"I know! See? It's perfect."

He coughed into his hand and, inclining his head with an air of cockiness, said, "I did know that, actually. Because I can speak French."

"Liar," Evangeline accused, now confident in her ability to determine when he jested.

"*Je ne plaisante. Je parler français.*"

"Oh," she started, her mouth open in surprise. Her confidence was obviously misplaced.

"And four other languages," he continued. "Besides English."

"Wow. I'm impressed. I didn't mean to call you a liar. I thought you were kidding around."

"I know."

"What are the other languages?"

"Portuguese, Italian, Spanish, and Catalan are the others I'm fluent in."

"I suddenly feel...inadequate. I only know a very little French."

30

He shrugged. "Nah. I'm no genius, my parents just started me on it early, so it's been easy for me to pick them up. My dad would speak Portuguese to me since I was a baby, so I grew up speaking it just like English. I started on the others a little later. They really encouraged it even though I'm sure they knew I was using a lot of cuss words and talking back."

Evangeline chuckled. "I'll bet. So your dad is from Portugal?"

"My dad's parents moved here from Brazil in the '50s. Supposedly my grandfather's father left Portugal with Pedro III during the Restoration. I say supposedly because I don't think my grandfather would have felt a need to emigrate if his dad was buddies with the Emperor. My grandmother was from an Italian family in Brazil, and my mom's side of the family is Italian and Swedish. They mostly came here before the Martians, but we still have a lot of relatives in 'the old country.' My parents are really into geneology and they found a bunch of distant cousins on the grid and they like to use me as their official translator. It's annoying."

"That's amazing. I know next to nothing about my family history."

"You never told me your last name," he said. "I guess I didn't, either. Mine's Pereira."

"You're right! How silly. My last name's Garver."

Sebastian Pereira inclined his head in thought. "Hmm…that's probably English, so… I'd take a wild guess and say you have a lot of Irish or Scotch in you."

31

"I knew that much," she confirmed. "I guess the freckles and red hair are a dead giveaway, huh?"

"Gosh, yes." Sebastian shivered theatrically. "I totally have a thing for gingers."

"Oh, really?" Evangeline was blushing yet again, and thrust her hands into her jacket pockets. She wondered if he was really flirting with her. It would have been obvious to anyone else listening in, but it was often the case that shy young girls found reasons to doubt.

Sebastian opened his mouth like he was going to say something, but the words died in his throat and he let out a long sigh, the cloud of steam from his mouth momentarily fogging his glasses. "Sorry," he muttered.

"Oh, about what?" Evangeline replied hurriedly. Now she wondered if he'd misinterpreted her reaction.

Sebastian hesitated. "Uh…about those girls back in the library. I'm sorry you had to deal with that."

"Oh, yeah." Evangeline's expression darkened at the memory. She had been enjoying their conversation so much that she'd nearly forgotten about it. "What was their deal? I don't think I even saw them before."

"Deal? That's just how they are. You didn't have bullies in Kansas?"

"Really? They're that nasty to just anybody? For no reason?"

"Genghis Cunt was jealous, and so she rallied her cronies to put you in your place."

Evangeline stared at Sebastian wide-eyed. For a moment the profane (and, she thought, apt) nickname stunned her into silence, but she soon burst out laughing. "Genghis…" she shook her head, not finishing the name.

Sebastian smirked. "That's what I like to call Vanessa DiPalmo and her pals. Genghis Cunt and her Mongolian Bitch Horde."

"Well chosen," Evangeline said. "But her being jealous of me? That's really nice of you to say so, but we both know she has nothing to be jealous about."

"What, you mean besides personality? You're at least as good-looking as her. The reason she looks so attractive is because she's always standing next to Angie 'the burn victim' Lasko and Larda Maxwell. Why do you think she keeps them around?"

"Oh boy, you have names for all of them," Evangeline laughed.

"Meh, Larda is too obvious to really take credit for. But you can't tell me Angie doesn't look like a burn victim with those ridiculous eyebrows."

He was right: she couldn't deny it, so she said nothing at all. Evangeline brushed her wind-swept hair out of her eyes and started pulling it back into a hasty ponytail. "I guess I should expect them to get even with me tomorrow, huh?"

"I wouldn't worry about it, Evangeline. If anything, they'll probably focus on me."

"Is that what you meant by catching hell over it?"

"They'll probably spread some stupid rumors. Genghis may try to get one of her boyfriends to beat me up."

"Oh, gosh, Sebastian! I'm so sorry I got you involved in this!"

"Well, you didn't. I did."

"Still…"

"I'm not worried about that stuff. But if any of the preceptors or the nuns overheard us, they'll probably go to my mom and dad and they'll…crap!"

"What's wrong?" Evangeline asked, feeling rather guilty.

"You said you live on Summerlea, right? I got so caught up in talking to you I forgot where we're going." He pivoted on his heel and was already walking in the other direction.

"Don't worry about it," she quickly put in as she followed. "What about your parents? I'd really hate for you to get in trouble over me." This was a *pro forma* lie, albeit unintentional; for even as she said the words she realized that the thought was flattering and exciting.

"I've been saving up to buy my mom's old car. It'd be just like them to call off the deal over this." Sebastian ground his teeth a little.

Evangeline was quick to volunteer her help. "If it would help at all, I would talk to them, tell them how it really happened!"

Sebastian looked at her out of the corner of his eye, smiling.

"It's the least I can do," she said.

"I may just have to take you up on that."

Sebastian led Evangeline home more quickly than she would have liked. They talked the whole way, their conversation effortless and pleasant. She found herself laughing a lot more than she was used to. When her house finally came into view over the lip of the hill, she thought about pretending not to notice where she was and keep on walking.

Then she spotted her dad's car along the curb and remembered that he wasn't working late tonight. Very briefly she considered introducing Sebastian to her father, but she doubted either of them would appreciate that.

"Well, I guess I'm home." The announcement came with such a dolorous tone that Sebastian eyed her curiously and Evangeline, surprised that her inner thoughts had crept so blatantly into her voice, let out a little embarrassed laugh.

"Thanks for walking me, Sebastian. And...for everything else."

He winked at her. "My pleasure, Evangeline."

"So...I guess I'll see you tomorrow?" she asked, backing up the stairs to her front door.

"I'll look for you. Oh! Wait!" He held up his wrist and pulled his sleeve up. A rectangle of glossy black plastic strapped to his wrist flashed in the fading sunlight. "Uhm, did you want to swap contact info? I don't know if you have your mobi on you..."

"Yeah! I do!" she replied excitedly, and hastily dug her own bodycomp out of her jacket pocket. She tapped it flat against his, and the two mobis chimed in sequence.

"Feel free to call or message me whenever!" Then, embarrassed by her own over-enthusiasm, she wished him a good night and ducked inside her house almost before he could reply.

Marshmallow was already purring and rubbing his back against her shin by the time she'd stepped through the foyer into the living room. Evangeline scooped the cat up off the ground and let out a squeak of happiness as she cradled him against her chest.

"I missed you today! Even though you got me in trouble!" she said, tapping him on his pink nose.

"Trouble? What kind of trouble?" Matthew Garver drew the question out slowly, sounding like a bored psychiatrist.

Evangeline started and leaped up from her crouch, and Marshmallow sprang from her arms onto the couch. She hadn't even noticed her father sitting at the table, half-obscured behind a levee of cardboard boxes that still hadn't been unpacked. She trotted over to him and kissed him on the cheek.

For a hundred reasons, she didn't feel like telling him about her encounter with Genghis Cunt and the Mongolian Bitch Horde. Fortunately, she knew from his tone of voice that he was feigning interest out of courtesy, so she wouldn't have to. "Nothing. I just had some cat hair on me, that's all."

He looked up from the mess of binders, protractors, and laminated data cloth on the table and stretched his long, tan arms over his head. "Ah, fashion trouble," he yawned.

Matthew stood up and leaned against the back of the chair as he sized up his daughter. "Well? How was this so-called school of yours?" There was a note of gentle mockery in his voice, and his shrewd grey eyes squinted at her in judgment. He viewed St. Bonaventure's pedagogical model, or lack thereof, skeptically and made no secret of it.

Evangeline thought back on Sebastian and smiled. "You know, it's a bit of getting used to, but I like it! I made a friend already!"

"Great! What's her name?"

"Sebastian. Uh, I think…" she hastily added, trying not to sound too interested.

Her father stroked his blond beard thoughtfully. "Hmm, doesn't sound like a girl's name to me."

She stuck her tongue out at him. "He's a boy, Dad. It's not a big deal."

"I hope you did something more than flirt with boys all day, Evangeline."

"Of course! Lots!"

"So tell me."

She hesitated, trying to put the confusion and idleness of her first day in a good light. "Well, they started off by showing me around the place. I talked to all of the preceptors, and they told me about their fields. I toured the workshops and listened in on a debate. I saw the chapel…and the gym…and…"

Her father waved her on. "So you gabbed a lot, and walked around. Right, right, go on."

She cocked her head and frowned at him. "And I spent a lot of time reading."

"I'm relieved you could work in something approximating education," he said.

"That's not fair, dad. It's my first day. I was sort of overwhelmed by everything."

"Are you going to do something more productive tomorrow? Besides tossing your hair and fluttering your lashes at Sebastian, I mean."

Evangeline did her best to ignore the snide comment. "Yes. One of the preceptors was a stage director and she's gathering ideas for the year-end play. And I can take drawing lessons, too!"

He made a sour face. "I guess that counts for something."

"Dad, come on! Not everybody has to be an engineer. I have no interest in that stuff and I'm not cut out for it anyway. I just didn't get your brains."

Matthew Garver's condescending expression straightened, his lips pressed together in a hard line. Evangeline saw the change and her shoulders slumped. She knew what was coming, wondered what she might say to defuse the situation, but she had no answers. She just wanted to get the fighting done with.

"What did I say now?" she whispered.

"You wouldn't take after me, would you? No, you are your mother's daughter." His voice was cold and distant; the statement laid on like a curse.

Evangeline's throat tightened and she felt the familiar sting in her eyes. "Huh? What does that mean?" She wished he would just work late all the time.

She remembered – and it didn't seem so long ago – when she felt like she was everything to her father. They would play and sing together and laugh at each other's corny jokes. And she remembered how he told her how proud she made him.

Now, every conversation was a battle and everything she did seemed a bitter disappointment to him. Now, she could talk more easily with a boy she'd known for a half-hour than with her own father. Now, she looked forward to his late nights at work because she could go to sleep without seeing his angry, suspicion-filled glances on the backs of her eyelids and wondering what she could have possibly done to merit them.

"What did I do wrong?" Evangeline desperately wanted an answer to that question. She spent long, painful hours locked up inside herself trying to figure it out.

She could time her father's resentment to the day he first learned that she was a talent. Evangeline expected that reaction, knew how uncomfortable, even afraid, it made many people. But she had also expected him to have gotten over it by now.

She feared that the problem was not thermokinesis or anything she'd done, but something deeper, something about who she was: A girl. A girl who reminded him of his ex-wife. The sound of her voice. Something unfixable.

Whatever it was, his silence told her he wasn't going to reveal it today. As she rubbed at her tears she said, "I don't know what you want me to do."

She felt the reassuring warmth of his hand on her back as he stepped forward and hugged her. "I'm sorry, Eva," he whispered. His eyes were closed and his chin rested on her head and he held her tight, and she lowered her arms and hugged him back.

"Forgive me," he said, and she knew he meant it. He still sometimes had these flickering moments of real tenderness.

But a flicker is all they were. There would be another fight tomorrow or maybe even tonight.

"Someone needs to look out for you, keep you on the right path, you know?" he said eventually, and the familiar harshness crept back into his voice. "You need me to be tough on you. Someday you'll understand."

She pulled away from him, sniffing back her tears. "I'm going to go finish my chores and then take a nap. I'm pretty tired."

"What about dinner? Don't you want-"

"I'm not hungry." Nauseous was more like it. She stooped to grab Marshmallow and hurried upstairs.

Close Encounters

I already knew there was going to be trouble tonight. I didn't know where or what kind, but I knew it. It had nothing to do with ESP, just one of those feelings anybody can get, a notion that sneaks inside your skull and curls up in a corner of your brain, periodically flashing its glowing eyes out of the darkness to remind you.

It was the start of the weekend, and I planned to be out late. I was at Close Encounters, the Shadyside night club with the retro-future motif, for the first under-18 night of the spring, and the place was packed. The glass on the windows hummed from the music (which sucked) and your head vibrated in resonance with the depleted Cavorite dance floor salvaged from the hull of a junked Martian blastboat. That was the big reason people went there: to make an ass of themselves in one-third G. In Martian gravity, everyone was light on their feet. And the subliminal pulsing did something, too. It made you euphoric, put you in a trance where every face was happy and every touch felt amazing, like broadcast ecstasy. Nobody really knew how it worked. Some people said it was psychosomatic, but that was a load of crap. Nine out of ten people would have felt it the first time they walked into the place without being told about it, and I'd give you even odds that the 10th person was either a void or a sociopath. There were almost never any fights at 'Encounters.

Almost.

I was sitting at a table against the wall, knocking back those fruity wine coolers the girls like along with Gil Benjamin and Rachel Mercado. This was against the law in Pennsylvania, and since it was under-18 night there wasn't even supposed to be any alcohol on the floor, but Rachel's aunt was one of the bartenders and she was decent enough to supply us. It felt strange being there with Rachel, my sometimes/almost girlfriend. I'd have preferred Evangeline's company, but even though I'd been flirting with her I hadn't actually ginned up the courage to ask her out. At first I thought that was why I felt anxious, but I was soon to be disabused of that idea.

It had only been three days since I met Eva, since I stuck up for her against Vanessa DiPalmo and her sycophants, and so far the other shoe hadn't dropped. I knew they were going to try to get even, but they hadn't tried to set me up with the dean and I hadn't even heard any nasty rumors circulating about me. I figured she'd forgotten about it, because I had. But that was stupid of me; women never give up a grudge.

Rachel had stepped away to mingle with some of her other friends and Gil and I were just talking — I don't remember what, baseball or something probably — when I saw his mouth kind of drop open and his eyeballs roll up, and I knew right then that trouble had finally arrived. I set my drink down and glanced over my shoulder just as a hand clamped down on it. The fingers dug deep into my trapezius muscle. I winced, holding my breath so I didn't yelp out loud.

42

"This is the guy?"

"That's the one, babe," Vanessa DiPalmo said. I could practically hear her smile.

"You look familiar," he breathed at me. I knew Steve Saranchuk well enough. He didn't go to St. Bonaventure, but he played Teener League ball. He was a good first baseman, and like most first basemen I knew he was an obnoxious bully. He stood a little taller than me and a lot burlier. More importantly, he had the drop on me, so I didn't say or do much right then. I didn't think I could count on Gil to back me up. If Alex had been there, I'm sure he'd have already drilled Saranchuk, but he wasn't, so it didn't matter. And even if he had been, it might not have turned out well for either of us; I saw the huge girth of Steve's best goon, Tommy Nowakowski, hemming me in on the other side. Tommy played baseball too, only he wasn't any good. He was a decent enough defensive lineman when he played football, but only by virtue of his giant size. He was well over six feet tall and almost as big around, a great deal of fat over a great deal of muscle.

"Pereira, isn't it?" he said, only he mangled the pronunciation, making it rhyme with 'cafeteria.' It probably wasn't intentional. That wasn't Saranchuk's kind of humor; he was just stupid. "Sounds like a disease. That's some kind of spic name, isn't it? Yeah, I remember you. Second baseman. Kind of a pussy. Liked to whine about getting spiked."

Remember what I said about sociopaths?

"I heard you've been shooting your mouth off at my woman. Insulting her and her lady friends, threatening them. Threatening ladies is the sort of a thing you'd expect from a limp-wristed pussy, isn't it? Well, Pereira, speak up."

I fought to keep myself from shaking, but you can't fight adrenaline. I was scared and furious, but right then I just wanted to get out of there without looking like a coward or getting my head beat in. He still had his hand dug into my shoulder and it hurt like hell. I didn't think I could turn around fast enough to do anything before one or both of them clobbered me. Part of me wanted to apologize, to say anything just to get him to leave, but thankfully my manlier sensibilities won out, and I just didn't say anything.

"Oh, I get it. Your mouth is only loose around ladies. You don't open it up around men because you know you'd get your head kicked in. You coward."

"Look at the little bitch sweat," Nowakowski added, grinning like he had gas.

There are limits to the degradation a man is willing to accept even when the alternative is sure physical harm, and I had reached mine. I was calculating my best first strike option, wondering if I could drive my foot into Tommy's balls and punch Saranchuk in the throat before they both tackled me. A fist fight is more about size and strength than anything else, but no one was too big or too tough to be beaten, so long as you were willing to be brutal and go for instant incapacitation. My main fear was that it would take too long for the dumb Polock to realize I kicked him in the nuts and he'd crush me in the meantime.

But it never came to that, because just as my muscles tightened to stand up and flip over the table, I was shocked by something cold and wet soaking

44

through my pants. My eyes rolled up to see Saranchuk's other hand holding my bottle of wine cooler, inverted. He let go of me then.

"There," he said, as Vanessa cackled behind him. "You were going to piss yourself anyway. Word to the wise: next time I have to talk to you, I'm just going to batter you. Understand me, boy?"

He dropped the bottle in my lap and they walked off into the crowd.

Gil stared across the table at me, pale and wide-eyed. "What was that about?"

"Nothing," I spit out, choking on my own humiliation. "Thanks for all your help."

"What was I supposed to do?" He must have known the answer to that question, though, because he looked ashamed. It wasn't his fault, and it wasn't his fight. I know that, but I hated his guts right then and I felt like diving across the table and beating the hell out of him. But there was a cold ember starting to flare inside me, and it said that if anyone was getting the hell beat out of him tonight, it was Steve Saranchuk. And it reminded me of something, else, too.

'You're a superhero.' I could almost hear it like another voice in my head. 'Make them afraid of you.'

I forced a smile over at Gil and offered my apologies. He accepted them readily, and offered some of his own.

"Don't sweat it," I said, and slid a few coins across the table. "Buy us another round while I clean myself up."

Then I got up and moved into the crowd, but I didn't go to the bathroom. I looked for Genghis and

45

her boyfriend. I found them at a tall table near the edge of the dance floor, and as luck had it Nowakowski was blundering over from the bar with a big pitcher of pop. I just had to smile, and I knew the Lord was smiling along with me.

I assure you that you have never seen a sober yonko have so much trouble with a beverage before. I was subtle with the hydrokinesis at first, and the pop sloshed around just enough to splash out on his hands and his cheeks. He stopped and slowed down a couple of times, thinking that he was walking too fast. That's when I really kicked it up. He swore as a geyser of cola and ice hit his face, and he flung the pitcher away in surprise and actually fell down. There was enough laughter you could actually hear it against the beat of the music, and that really steamed him. A couple of kind souls bent down to help him, but he cursed them and shook them off. The pitcher was made of glass, but it was one of those heavy, tempered ones, so it didn't shatter; he retrieved it and went back to the bar for a refill.

So I did it again, and I soaked his shirt till it was brown and his flabby man-tits stuck out. Vanessa mocked him ruthlessly and Saranchuk angrily yanked the pitcher out of his hands and told him to sit down. "You've wasted enough of my money!" I heard him say.

"That glass is haunted!" Nowakowski replied. He held out his dripping arms and looked down at himself pitifully.

I didn't let Saranchuk fare any better. I waited until he was looking straight ahead at the table and sloshed the whole pitcher right down the front of his body. He, too, dropped the pitcher and stood there in utter shock. Even the bartender yelled over the noise, "What? Again?" The crowd roared with laughter. I watched with great joy as Vanessa's face twisted in humiliation and she tried to hide behind her hand.

One of the waitresses came out with a mop and bucket, and the crowd cleared out from around the spill, leaving a wide open avenue between me and Saranchuk. My hand started shaking again, and that cold ember blazed into naked heat. That was enough playing around.

My shoes squelched as I crossed the sticky floor, and I bent down to grab the pitcher, still half-filled with ice, then came up right beside him. As soon as he turned his head, I smashed the pitcher into his jaw. He reeled backwards and his feet kicked out on the slick floor and he went down like a bag of wet shit.

The next thing I knew, there was an arm around my neck, a steel coil coated in fat, hurling me into the dance floor. My legs went up in the air and I spun around backwards, but I didn't come down immediately. As my body crossed the contragravity envelope, I glided across the air for yards and slowly drifted down to the floor, like the air itself was fighting me. It was one of the most surreal things I'd ever experienced. And that pulsing, the resonance of the field against my skull, was even more pronounced. My brain felt like jello. I was giddy; I actually laughed as my shoulders softly hit the ground.

But then that fat Polock fell on me, and it wasn't so funny anymore. Even at a third of a G, it wasn't

47

very pleasant to have his elbow come down on my gut and drive all the air out of my lungs. Nowakowski recovered pretty quickly, and he got his paws around my neck and started to squeeze and slam my head into the ground simultaneously. I guess the low gravity saved me, because he couldn't quite get enough leverage to really crack my skull, but he was doing a fine job choking me. My limbs flailed, anything I could to get him off me. Finally my thrashing knee connected with his groin. My suspicions about him being too stupid to feel it were disproved, and the hand he'd held on my throat immediately slackened. Nowakowski moaned hoarsely as I threw him off me. I hopped to my feet to stomp on him, but then another set of arms circled my waist, yanking me off my feet and rushing me off the dance floor. It was the bouncer, and he obviously had a lot more skill at moving across the Cavorite than any of us did. I could see the other bouncers rounding up Nowakowski and Saranchuk, whose head wobbled around on his neck while blood streamed from his nostrils.

I was deposited ungently on the pavement and told to get lost. The manager, a perpetually sunburned, middle-aged guido came out screaming, his veins sticking out from the collar of his polo shirt. "You delinquents are banned FOR LIFE! Do you understand me?"

I looked up at him and the bouncer separating me from Saranchuk and Nowakowski, who were being shooed in the opposite direction. I nodded and shrugged. Fair enough. It was worth it.

"Now get out of here before I call the Troubleshooters!" the manager screamed again, then slammed the front door.

As I got up, I saw Vanessa run out the front door, bawling her eyes out, with Rachel and Gil close behind her. Despite having been humiliated, nearly choked to death, and banned for life, I was feeling pretty good about myself. Vindicated, you might say. Then Rachel cuffed me on the head.

"Sebastian, you super giant asshole! What the hell is the matter with you?" she screamed at me.

"They started it. I'll vouch for that," Gil said. He patted me on the shoulder and gave me an admiring nod of the head.

"Apologize to your aunt for me, OK, Rach?" I said as I drifted away from them. "Go back and enjoy yourself and I'll see you on Monday. I have to go home and wash my pants."

Grimalkin

Taken day by day, the life of a masked vigilante is kind of boring. Between the big showdowns, the busted capers, and the close brushes with death, there's a lot of waiting for trouble, and most often trouble doesn't trouble to happen. The truth is there's an awful lot of running around for what seems like no good reason. At least that's the way it is with me, here in the 'Burgh.

Once in a while, though, you stumble into something worth talking about. Let me tell you about one of those times.

This was only a little while after I unexpectedly expressed during the fight with the spraypaint vandals. My scrapes and black eyes were healed and I had been back in action for a little while. I had updated my outfit to something that looked a little less like it came from a burglar's wardrobe by adding some bright blue trim and trading in the ski mask for a hooded sweatshirt that I stitched an eye mask onto. After too much trouble getting the eyeholes to stay in one place, I bought a pair of slick-looking smart goggles to hold the mask in place. I was starting to look like a real superhero.

Alex had joined me on two patrols, but he wasn't with me this night, probably because it was getting terminally boring. But I was confident that a change of scenery would fix that.

You see, the first time I put on the mask, I went out thinking that I would strictly focus on neighborhood, the way Technophile sticks to the

North Side, or how in Meridian Harbor nearly every covenant community has a superhero. But now it was obvious that there just wasn't enough crime in my part of Shadyside to merit even a part-time vigilante. If I wanted to be more than the talent equivalent of a mall rent-a-cop, I'd have to go where life was dangerous. I'd have to go to the wrong side of the tracks. Literally.

A railroad spur cuts through a place called Panther Hollow, near Schenley Park, forming the boundary between the Oakland and Squirrel Hill neighborhoods. From there it runs to a big Chesapeake & Kanawha switching yard along the northern bank of the Monongahela, which, at that location, forms a fat bulge almost half as wide as Squirrel Hill. Despite being such a big open area, there's almost nothing there besides the switching yard: no people, no buildings, not even any trees or grass. Everyone calls it The Blight. Supposedly it was poisoned by the Martians during the siege a hundred years ago and it's never been fit for living things to grow there since then; sort of like what happened to Baltimore, I guess. It's about the bleakest place in Pittsburgh.

Bordering the Blight, just above the limit of the contamination where brown scrub grass and stunted, sickly looking trees can grow, is the remains of the old neighborhood of Hazelwood. Some of the first homesteads in the city were built there, and once upon a time it was tidy and peopled with salt-of-the-earth types. Now, Hazelwood is poor, run-down, and crime-ridden, and the only people who live there are those who can't get out. The Blight and the railroad tracks keep it relatively isolated from the rest of the city, and although some folks may say otherwise, that's just the way the rest of the city wants to keep it. At the time, I thought that maybe all the place needed was a superhero — but I was pretty naive back then.

I left my house at midnight and rode my bike through Greenfield, passing through the wide wooded gap that divided Hazelwood from the rest of the city. I remembered the woods looking pretty from the crests of the hills in Schenley Park, but right then they felt a lot creepier, even threatening. The night was nearly moonless and inky dark, and the breadth of the wood, though no more than a quarter mile in reality, looked endlessly deep and primeval. Worse was the way the dense growth deadened all the normal sounds of the city. I pedaled my fastest to get through it, eager for the familiar glow of electric lights and the hum of traffic.

Hazelwood, as I have said, is a dump, and as I zoomed past the first few blocks of dilapidated houses I felt that I had judged the creepy woods too harshly. This part of the neighborhood seemed every bit as desolate. Three of the first four street lamps I passed were busted, and the few windows that weren't boarded up were knocked out, revealing long-abandoned interiors. A little further on, I began to see signs of human activity: for instance, the jalopy that ran a red light at 40 miles per hour, missing my back tire by a nose hair and nearly bringing a promising vigilante career to a premature end. The four fine specimens in the car thrust out various body parts and shouted their opinions about "bike-riding queers." Their unique dialect only barely resembled the

English with which I was familiar, so I allow that I might have missed their apology.

I coasted down a narrow side street, hopped off my bike and just crouched for a minute on shaking legs, trying to compose myself. All of a sudden, I heard an awful inhuman screeching. I ran in the direction of the sound halfway down the block when I heard it again, louder this time. It sounded like a cat being skinned alive. And I say that because, well...

I looked across an overgrown, rubble-strewn lot, where a row house used to be. Within the decayed ruin of the foundation were four men, probably about my age judging by their slang and the way they dressed. One of them had a long knife in one hand, and in the other the back legs of a flailing cat.

I can't tell you exactly what happened next. Hell, I might not even have known what I was doing as I did it. The only thing I'm certain of is that I gave no warning, said nothing at all until I was right on top of the one with the knife. I had him on the dirt, was straddling his ribs. He had to have dropped the knife and the cat because he was waving both of his bloody hands in front of his face, trying to ward off my fists. I used both arms, and I used them until my lungs burned and pain shot up from my split knuckles, and even then I went on pounding. I think a hand grabbed my hood and tried to drag me back, but I flung an elbow and the pulling stopped, and I went back to punching for what seemed like hours. More than once I missed that ugly head and pounded my fists straight into the ground. Eventually something hard bounced off the front of my skull and knocked me off of him. I squeezed my eyes shut from the pain and rolled sideways, instinctively trying to avoid another attack. I felt the gash rippling on my forehead and the blood seeping into my mask. For the first time, I remembered that I had powers, but my head hurt too badly to use them. Then I remembered the telescoping stun baton on my waist. I ripped it from the holster, flicked my wrist to bring it to full extension. My finger tightened on the trigger as I blindly swung it around me. I could hear the whipcracks of electricity slinging from probe to probe, see the ultra bright flashes of minute thunderbolts through my closed eyes.

When I finally got back to my feet and opened my eyes, there wasn't anybody there to hit. I saw the the limping, bleeding cat and the fragments of cinder block that broke against my head. Aside from some footprints in the moist clay, there was no sign of the quartet of teenage sociopaths, not even the one I had pinned.

I got lucky again. Damn lucky. It was almost a repeat of the fight with the vandals. I went off half-cocked, not thinking, not even making the most of the tools I had with me. If the creep I tackled hadn't dropped his blade, or if one of the other ones had picked it up, they might have buried it in my ribs. Or that cinder block might have been aimed from the back at the soft part of my skull and I might have gone down for good.

But some things you just react to, and there's no helping it.

I'm a dog guy, never really liked cats. But the deep and true parts of me were not about to stand there and let that happen, even if stopping it cost me the farm. Cruelty to animals ate at me in a way that cruelty to other people just didn't. I believe I was mad enough that if those monsters had stuck around, I might have murdered them, and only a little faster than the way they were trying to murder that cat.

The cat hissed and swiped at me when I bent down next to it, but the poor thing was too injured and weak to get away. I cradled it against my chest, stroked its back softly where the bloody fur was already matting together. I hushed it and told it that everything was going to be alright, though I had no idea how badly he was injured or where I could go for help at that hour.

As I was wondering about that, something moved across my peripheral vision. For the instant my eyes caught it, I saw that it was big, the size of a man at least. The sociopaths were coming back to fight, after all. I trotted backwards, still holding the cat close, and bent down to grab the shock stick.

'No,' I thought. 'Can't be them.' I belatedly realized that the figure, whatever it was, seemed to be loping along on four legs. It was probably a neighborhood dog on the loose. The cat hissed and yowled again, as if in sudden fear.

"Relax, buddy, you'll be okay," I whispered.

Something crunched with a heavy tread on the loose dirt behind me and the air filled with the roar of a hungry cougar. You hear that bloodcurdling cry once in a movie or at the zoo, and it stays with you for the rest of your life.

The wildly thrashing cat slipped out of my grasp when I spun around. I didn't look down to pick it back up, and I am ashamed to say that for several hours I did not think of that cat at all. And that sound I heard, the thing that stood before me poised to pounce, was not a mountain lion.

I told you I couldn't remember everything that happened in the fight, but I can paint you a picture of the thing and not leave out a single detail, from the sickly yellow color of the saliva that dripped from its bear-trap mouth to the mottled grey folds of its wrinkled skin. Its whiskered, blunt-snouted skull towered more than a foot above my head. The thing stood up on two legs, though the legs were jointed in the wrong direction for a man, like the hind paws of a quadruped. The creature was mostly hairless with scattered patches of matted fur, like it had mange. Maybe it resembled a Sphynx cat, but only if Sphynx were seven feet tall with the jaws of a jaguar and long, human fingers. Let's call a spade a spade and get it out of the way: I was staring down a werecat.

The beast hissed through its yellow fangs and slashed at me. I don't know how it missed me because it was so close I felt its breath on my neck, but miss me it did, and I ran for my life. I ran past where I'd left my bike and had to double back in a panic. Once more I saw it leap out from around the corner of the empty lot, bounding towards me on all four legs. I jumped on the bike, switched on the electric assist, and shot out onto the main street without even a thought about oncoming traffic. My leg muscles were already on fire, but I didn't stop pedaling until I was more than halfway home and the hills were too steep and too frequent to conquer. I glided home on the motor and prayed to God that I had been hallucinating.

56

It was quarter to two when I got back home. Luckily, nobody was awake to see me stagger through the back door in my Torrent costume, forehead caked with dried blood. I tested the locks on every door and window before limping up to my bedroom, and I locked that door, too.

A little while later, I got up the nerve to go to the bathroom and clean myself up. The cut wasn't that bad after I washed all the blood away, though I had a noticeable lump. I cleaned and bandaged the cut and mostly forgot about it. The werecat was another matter entirely.

I was too tuned up with adrenaline – and fear – to try sleeping, so I spent the rest of the night in my room trying to come to terms with what I'd seen. I wanted a rational explanation for it. I wondered if it might not have been a really intense flash of psychometry, but I quickly dismissed that idea. What the hell sort of memory would that have been? And besides, I had never had a psychometric impression that was so completely indistinguishable from my own vision.

I turned to the Grid for answers. If you've ever searched for 'werecat,' you know the sort of obscene garbage I had to wade through. The first thing I found that made any sense and wasn't drawn from the perverse fantasies of a disturbed teenager suggested that I had run into a Moreau. It seemed obvious, and I didn't know why I didn't think of it before. But the more I thought about it, the less convinced I became. The human-animal hybrids were rare: Life Haven, a clade that advocates for Moreau rights, estimated their population to be less than 10,000 in the whole world.

They also tended to live amongst their own kind, in small isolated communities in rural areas. It wasn't out of the question that there might be some wild, atavistic Moreau on the loose in Hazelwood, but it seemed unlikely.

I followed some other tracks, but most of what I found was hearsay, light on facts and big on credulous speculation. At the other end of the spectrum, and of equally little help, were the scoffers: the Houdini Center admitted no knowledge of shapeshifters or therianthropy, and called it delusion and superstition. The most interesting thing I found that night was on the gridnode of a small paranormal research group from New Jersey, the Institute for Metaphysical and Phenomenological Studies (makes a cute acronym, doesn't it?). They provided the case files of the late Dr. John Silence, the famous psychic investigator. Two of these, both from the 1920s, seemed relevant. In the first, Silence and his assistant Hubbard directly encounter a shapeshifter on an isolated island in the Baltic Sea. Silence explained the wild wolf form as, I crap you not, the ectoplasmic nocturnal emissions of a sexually frustrated teenager. You think that sounds absurd? So did I, but the evidence he put forward made a believer out of me.

What I didn't know then, what I couldn't have known until I first got slimed by Meryl, was that this theory couldn't explain what I encountered, since ectoplasm lights up my Eerie – my sixth sense – like a lightbulb. The sensation is overwhelming. I didn't get anything like that. To tell the truth, I don't remember getting any psychometric impressions at all.

Silence's second case dealt with the remarkable account of an unremarkable man, an English nebbish named Arthur Vezin, who minutely describes his capture by, and narrow escape from, a Satanic cult of humanoid werecats in a rural French hamlet. Vezin's account is frankly terrifying, but Dr. Silence wasn't much impressed by it. After an uncharacteristically terse investigation into Vezin's background and a visit to the town of the alleged French werecats, Silence wrote off the event as entirely hallucinatory, the product of an overstressed man's delusional break with reality. I was miffed at this curt dismissal of a horrifically vivid and earnest account, probably in large measure because I imagined Dr. Silence making the same verdict about my adventure in Hazelwood. But he would have been dead wrong. I wasn't overstressed, I never thought about werecats, and I sure as hell wasn't a nebbish.

But I began to doubt myself, and the doubt set my thinking down a fruitful path. My recollections of the beast seemed so surreal, almost like they'd been superimposed on my memories. Why was the image of the cat-thing so clear in my mind? The night had been so dark, and the lot was half in shadow even from the nearby streetlight. Hadn't it been dark enough that the four punks didn't see me come upon them until it was too late? Hadn't it been too dark for one of them to pick up the knife and use on me? And it was so dark that I couldn't even see their faces, except for the one I was right on top of. How could the werecat have stood out so distinctly, as if I'd run into it in broad daylight?

It dawned on me that I couldn't have seen what I thought I saw, the way I thought I saw it. I wasn't delusional, but that didn't mean I wasn't hallucinating.

At dawn, I girded my loins and went back out to investigate my hypothesis, but this time I went as Sebastian Pereira, not Torrent. Physically, I was exhausted, but my brain was racing too fast to let me sleep. Besides, the evidence I was looking for wouldn't wait around for a nap.

Downstairs, my dad was already up; a disgusting habit brought on by youth on a farm and an adulthood as an entrepreneur. He was sitting at the kitchen table and looked up at me over the rim of a cup of coffee so black it would've woken six out of seven Ephesian martyrs by scent alone. "Noon already?" he said, dryly.

"Well timed and expertly delivered. I actually haven't gone to sleep yet."

"What happened to your head?"

"Oh, nothing much. Some delinquents hit me with a brick," I said, trying to sound arch.

He sighed and shook his head. "There's barely room enough for one wiseass in this house, son."

'I knew that would work', I thought, smiling. 'Well, if the truth isn't good enough...'

"I fell off my bike," I said. "I don't think it's bad, but I wasn't going to risk a coma by going to sleep."

He gave my head a good look-over. Satisfied, he said, "I should have never let your mother teach you to ride a bike. Where are you going?"

"Just wanted to check up on something before I sleep the afternoon away."

He shot me a stern look. "You promised you'd take care of the yard work today."

"I promised you the yard work would get done, not specifically that I would do it," I corrected him. "Don't worry, it'll get done. See you later."

In retrospect, I went out rather unprepared; I even forgot my stun baton. But I was counting on the daylight reducing to a minimum the incidence of werecats and random street violence. Fortunately, I made it to the lot without anyone bothering me or even trying to run me over. I jumped down into the dugout from the sidewalk and sniffed around for tracks.

The clay soil was wet and the impressions of feet and other indentations were well preserved in the soft, bare ground. I recognized my boot prints and the treads of many sneakers, the paw prints of dogs, and in a couple of different spots I saw what I thought were some clumps of bloody fur from the poor housecat. Absolutely nowhere did I see the monster footprints required of a seven-foot-tall ailuranthrope. Unless that thing was literally covering its tracks (and why would it bother?), it could not have been a Moreau or a manbeast of any sort. Even an ectoplasmic construct would've had to leave tracks commensurate with its mass and the shape of its feet.

I went home and had my sleep, but not before slipping $5 to my enterprising 12-year-old neighbor to get the lawn mowed. At nightfall, I visited Hazelwood again as Torrent. Besides my usual kit, I packed a jar of holy water blessed by Father Dan last Easter and a silver serving dish that I slipped, unnoticed, from the china cabinet, just in case my hunch was wrong. Admittedly, I had no idea if any of that stuff really worked, but hey, this job is more art than science. And before I left, I beseeched the intercession of St. Michael by the prayer that had never yet failed me, calling upon him to defend me in battle and to thrust Satan into Hell, and all his pals with him.

I felt prepared and confident of everything but how I could get the attention of my nemesis.

Hours passed as I staked out the lot and cycled loops around the neighborhood, but there were no monster cat people to be found. There was no other obviously nefarious activity either, though I sighted a dozen instances of *malum prohibitum* that I could have cracked down on if I was the type of dogwhistle to do things like that (here's looking at you, Crimebuster!). I was getting worried that someone might rob an all-night convenience store and I'd have to call off the hunt. Then an idea came to me.

I walked up and down the darkened backstreets around the empty lot. The street was still, quiet, and I thought most of the buildings were abandoned. I dialed up the little speakers on my mobi as far as they'd go and started playing recordings of mewling cats that I found on the Grid. Nothing stirred save for a few cats whose eyeglow I spied on top of ledges and behind piles of garbage. For about ten minutes I went on walking and playing the sounds, and then I decided to play something a little more extreme: a recording of a pair of cats fighting. Their frenzied, shrill screams were startlingly loud in the calm silence of the main streets, and even I jumped at them, momentarily surprised.

63

My Eerie buzzed, low and subtle at first. Immediately, I heard the rapid patter of a heavy tread – no alley cat, this one – and that heart-stopping roar.

I spun around, the extended shock-stick in my right hand and the jar of holy water in my left, and watched the beast lope down the alley toward me. It was huge and slavering, its glowing eyes leaving a green trail in the darkness as its head bobbed. I told myself that I mustn't panic, that it wasn't real – but all my certainty and self-confidence flew away like a balloon with the air let out once I saw those four-inch claws spring out of its paws.

I thrust out the baton at the same time I flung the holy water, all the while psychically dragging the spray of liquid into the beast's eyes. I felt contact on the end of the rod and then it reeled back, yowling and hissing. Then that animal screeching started to sound a lot like a screaming woman.

The werecat was gone: it was there one instant, and just flashed out of existence the next. On the ground in front of me was a bony woman with damp, dirty blonde hair and an expression of horror on her deeply creased face. She looked so despondent and helpless that I pitied her despite all the adrenaline pumping through my veins. I stopped the juice and yanked the baton back.

My hunch had been right. It was just a telepathic illusion, not a real werecat – if there even were such things – and 100,000 volts was enough to disrupt her broadcast. That's why I could see the details so clearly even in the dark, and why it left no tracks in the mud, or at least no inhuman tracks. Only I had suspected it was one of the cat-skinning lowlifes I chased away last night, not this terrified, middle-aged lady in dingy, frumpy clothes.

"He was my cat!" she cried – cried literally, anguished tears pouring down her cheeks. She was shaking, choking with rage and misery. "Why?!" she screamed again. "Why?! He was so sweet! He never hurt anyone!"

"Oh, God." I breathed, more a prayer more than an exclamation. "It wasn't me. I-I tried to stop them. I don't know who they were. Is your cat...?"

I couldn't finish the sentence, but the way she started sobbing right then I knew what the answer was and I knew I didn't care for it. I dropped the empty bottle and the stick and walked over beside her. She recoiled from me as I bent down to help her up. I felt ashamed and disgusted.

"I'm sorry," I said, and cringed at how useless that sounded, but I said it again. "I'm sorry I hurt you. I'm sorry for what they did to your cat."

She punched me weakly in the chest and broke loose. I watched her run down the alley and disappear into the shadows.

'My first victory against another talent,' I thought, and laughed mirthlessly. What a sick, sad joke.

And I wished I knew where to find those four teenagers.

The Marshmallow Roast

"So, I know we spend so much time together here that you're probably sick of me, but I wanted to invite you to my house tomorrow night for supper." Evangeline let out a sharp exhale as she finished, like she'd been holding her breath a long time.

Sebastian blinked at her from across the table, noting her increasing agitation and embarrassment the longer he delayed his reply. Unfortunately, she had begun just as his teeth closed around a forkful of bison and he was now in the awkward position of deciding which breach of etiquette would be worse.

Before he had time to swallow, or even a reasonable chance to try speaking with his mouth full, she blurted, "I mean, if you're not busy, of course. And if you're *not* actually sick of me."

"I'd be delighted! Supper sounds wonderful! Thanks!" Alex Shepherd interjected and smiled toothily.

Evangeline let out a nervous squeak and bit her lower lip. "Oh, uh, I…actually…"

Alex shook his head. "Relax, I knew who you were talking to."

Sebastian finally swallowed his food. "Of course I'm not sick of you, Eva. That'd be great. Would you like me to bring anything?"

"Oh, no! I'll take care of everything. All you have to do is tell me what you'd like." Evangeline produced a piece of folded, laminated cardboard from her backpack and handed it over to Sebastian, who studied it quizzically.

"Uh, this is the Allegheny Grill menu," he noted.

"Oh, yes. I started waiting tables there, and I asked them if I could bring home meals every so often if they took it out of my paycheck," Evangeline explained. "Do you dislike their food?"

"No, not at all. I think their food is good. It's just that I, um, thought you were going to cook," Sebastian replied.

Evangeline's freckled cheeks turned red and she let out a nervous chuckle. "Oh, I'd never do that to you."

***

Sebastian stood on Evangeline's porch dressed in gray slacks and a cream-colored dress shirt, unbuttoned at the collar, underneath a suede dress jacket, a favorite of his wardrobe. All in all, his outfit was not greatly different than the sort of clothes he usually wore at St. Bonaventure. The main difference was in the care he took with it: pants neatly pressed, cheeks close-shaved, hair combed and styled, a touch of cologne. At school he dressed to meet the minimum requirements, tonight he dressed to look handsome. His left hand held a bouquet of flowers - daisies, the cheapest blooms he could purchase. Before ringing, he took a closer look around at the neighborhood. He did not see her father's car, which excited him.

Evangeline answered the ring of the doorbell almost immediately. She was a striking sight in her hip-hugging, ankle-length floral dress, orange heels and glittering earrings. She wore her hair pulled back in a neat bun, with only a few bouncing strands of red spiraling down over her forehead and her temples. She looked like a totally different woman, and Sebastian was almost humbled by her elegance and beauty. Almost.

"My God, Miss Garver!" he gasped. "You look almost as good as me."

She laughed. "You flatter me, Mr. Pereira."

Sebastian presented her the bouquet, and she accepted them glee. "Thank you! They're beautiful! But I told you not to bring anything."

He shrugged. "What kind of dinner guest would I be if I didn't?"

"You're early," she said, but she did not look or sound disappointed. "I hoped you would be! Now we have some time to talk before my dad comes home." She tugged him in by the wrist and shut the door. The house was warm, but Sebastian was feeling hot.

"So your dad will be joining us." Sebastian tried to make it sound like that was what he expected all along and was merely looking for confirmation. With some luck, Evangeline might even perceive it as him being considerate of her reputation, rather than the bleak disappointment and consternation that it actually was.

She nodded as she led him deeper into the narrow townhouse and offered a seat on the living room sofa. The house was smaller than what he imagined, primarily relying on his own home as a reference, but its tasteful and uncluttered furnishings made it feel cozy rather than cramped. Either

Evangeline had done a lot of preparatory cleaning beforehand, or Sebastian comparatively lived like a pig. He plopped down on the end of the sofa and waited until Evangeline returned from the kitchen with the flowers in a glass vase. She placed them in a position of honor on the coffee table and sat down very gently and ladylike on the middle cushion beside him.

"My dad would kill me if I had a boy over when he wasn't around. And he'd find out, too." She added playfully, "All it takes is one nosy neighbor, and there goes your reputation. No decent young man would want to be seen with me again!"

Sebastian smirked. "Your virtuousness is admirable, Eva, but I think you might be exaggerating just a tiny bit."

Evangeline shrugged and her voice took on a more serious tone. "Maybe things are different here. But where we last lived in Deseret, everybody noticed things like that, and word got around fast."

"That sounds terrible," Sebastian said.

Evangeline chuckled. "Well, it wasn't like the Transnistrian Secret Police or anything. I don't know, maybe it's a good thing. Most of the people were pretty well behaved out there."

Abruptly the tone and topic changed.

"Sebastian, thank you so much for coming. I know we're not, uhm, dating or anything, and it may seem a little weird to come here and have dinner with my dad and me, but I've mentioned you a bunch of times and he insisted that he meet you. He gets very curious about the company I keep. I don't want him to get upset over nothing and forbid me to hang out with you, or something extreme like that."

Throughout her speech, Sebastian's temples pounded like the drumbeat of doom. He did his best to take it in stride, however.

"Eva, I'm honored that you invited me. Your father just sounds like he's being a father. I totally understand why he'd want to protect his daughter." It wasn't a lie, exactly, but Sebastian was not nearly so comfortable with the scenario as he made it sound. And he must have made it sound convincing, too, considering Evangeline's reaction.

"No, you don't understand," Eva said, bowing her head. "I guess what I mean is that my dad can be very overbearing. And abrasive. And critical. In fact, he's kind of a jerk." She grabbed Sebastian's hand and looked him square in the eyes as she emphasized: "Sebastian, he's going to be mean to you. He's going to ask you all kinds of nosy questions and say all kinds of things that are going to make you mad, but please, please, please, for my sake, don't let it get to you. And try not to hate either of us after this is all over."

Sebastian couldn't help laughing, but it was the humor of the gallows. He tugged at the collar of his shirt, which suddenly felt very tight despite being unbuttoned. "What did you get me into here, Eva?"

"It's exhausting to be cooped up here every night, but if we can put him at ease, he'll let me off the leash a little bit. And I really need to get out of this house more often, and not just for school and CYO!" she replied.

Sebastian nodded and steeled himself for the coming struggle. He hoped he hadn't entirely lost his appetite. He saluted her and said, "I'll do my best, ma'am."

"Thank you! Now, tell me how you got that." Evangeline pointed to his forehead, where the scar from the impact with the cinder block was visible beneath his bangs. He'd gotten it stitched and it was healing well, but there was no hiding it.

Sebastian laughed. "I already told you, I got hit with a brick."

"Seriously, Sebastian! My dad's going to notice it, and if you give a smart aleck answer like that, he's not going to think it's funny. He'll think you're a thug!"

"Uh, Eva, I…I really did get hit with a brick," he said.

Her eyes went wide. "Well then you *definitely* can't tell him that! Make up something, quick!"

"Relax. I'll just say that I…fell from my bike. How's that?"

"Bicycle," she corrected. "If you say bike, he might think motorcycle."

He shook his head, but he was smiling. "Alright then…" but his voice trailed off into an inarticulate yell, and he leaped to his feet in sudden terror. As he stood flat against the wall catching his breath, the frightened white cat that had been catapulted off his lap scurried over to Evangeline and stared back at him in fluffy-eyed fear.

"Oh my gosh, are you alright?" She stood up, cradling and stroking the cat as she revealed it to him.

"It's OK, it was just Marshmallow! You're not afraid of cats, are you?"

Sebastian had the good grace to look embarrassed. He shook his head unsteadily. Afraid of cats? Him? Not exactly, though he had obviously not fully gotten over encountering a 'werecat' in Hazelwood last weekend.

"I'm really sorry, I don't know why I yelled like that. He just startled me," Sebastian apologized.

"Oh, I can put him in his pen for the rest of the night if he bothers you," Evangeline offered.

"No, no! It's his house, not mine!" Sebastian reached out to pet him, hopefully making amends for his rude greeting. "I'm sorry, buddy...what did you say his name was?"

"Marshmallow." She moved his front paw to wave at Sebastian and added, in a silly voice, "Sorry to frighten you, sir. I know that I'm an impressive cat!"

"You sure are, Marshmallow. And so puffy and fluffy! You remind me of a puppy I used to know! He was my best friend when I was a boy." Sebastian said.

"I didn't know you had a dog!" Evangeline said. "What was his name?"

Sebastian hesitated, a little embarrassed. "His name was Fwuffers, actually. He was a big white Husky and he shed all the time."

"Fwuffers!" Evangeline squealed. "What an adorable-!" But she stopped abruptly, and her head turned to the doorway at the sound of feet scuffling on the steps. Sebastian's eyes lingered on her, and he noted the expression of barely restrained dread on her face and the way she swallowed heavily as the latch to the deadbolt turned.

In walked her father, tall, svelte, and grumbling. He scowled as he unbuttoned his long brown trenchcoat and slammed the door shut with his foot. "You brought dinner home, I smell," he said without turning around. There was such a profound cheerlessness to his voice that Sebastian almost wanted to laugh.

"To what do I owe this pleasure?" he asked as he walked into the living room, then blinked in surprise at Sebastian, his words trailing off.

Sebastian shifted uncomfortably, shrugging his shoulders as if it could help him bear the weight of the older man's gaze. Her father stared at him forever, measuring and weighing him. Then, with the way the man's eyebrows crawled up his forehead and the slow, disgusted way he let out his breath, he delivered his judgment.

"Who's this?" he asked, turning to his daughter.

"D-dad, this is Sebastian," she squeaked. "You said we should have him over for dinner. Remember?"

"Oh, yes," he said. "I remember."

'Better late than never,' thought Sebastian. He bit the inside of his cheeks to keep from scowling.

"Sebastian, this is my dad, Matthew."

"Oh, he can call me Mr. Garver," Matthew laughed.

Sebastian winced, but he forced a flimsy smile and extended his hand just the same. "It's good to meet you. Mr. Garver." Matthew Garver seized

73

Sebastian's hand the way a gorilla might, and held it still instead of shaking it.

"Welcome to my home, Sebastian…?"

"Pereira."

Matthew finally released his grip on the younger man's hand. His eyes shifted to the kitchen, then over to his daughter as he stroked his thick blond beard thoughtfully. "So recipes from the back of a soup can are good enough for your dad, but not the boys at school, eh?"

Evangeline took the slight in stride. Indeed, she laughed along with her father. "Told you I wasn't much of a cook," she said to Sebastian.

"Oh well," Sebastian said, and he winked at her. "Everybody's got to have one flaw, I guess." She smiled at him bashfully.

The food, complements of the Allegheny Grill, was tasty if a bit drier than usual from being reheated. At any rate, it was a lot better than the table conversation. Sebastian was a fast eater, but he had to field so many questions he was worried his dinner would get cold. Questions about everything from where he lived to what his father did for a living and how he planned to make a living himself, each phrased and received judgmentally. Matthew even asked him, point blank, if he'd ever been arrested.

"Dad!" Evangeline exclaimed, her first words of protest against the increasingly inquisitorial proceedings.

Sebastian tried to play to his strengths of wit and humor. "Only once, but I was eventually acquitted." Unfortunately, the jest did not go over well. In fact, all of his jokes fell flat. Eva was too upset or cowed by her father to laugh, and Matthew wasn't amused. Sebastian felt both insulted and suffocated. Twenty five minutes into the meal, his appetite had evaporated and every bite was drudgery.

Something else bothered him, too. Sebastian had a vague feeling that he'd run into Matthew Garver before. He tried desperately to remember the context, wondering if the man's relentlessness was brought on by more than just protectiveness of his daughter. Had he seen Sebastian doing something unseemly? Had Sebastian insulted him? There must be something.

Eventually it clicked mid-way through one of Matthew's brief comments about his work advising Seneca Gas on a new shale oil extraction project. He was a mining engineer by trade.

"Excuse me, Mr. Garver," Sebastian interrupted him in the middle of his story. "Are you the same Matthew Garver that worked with Geo Templeton?"

Matthew slowly set down his fork and wiped his lips on a napkin. "I worked alongside George Templeton, yes."

"You were in the Compass Society!" Sebastian almost slammed his fist on the table in excitement. "You were on the Cibola expedition in Mojave! And you helped design the *Subterrene*, if I recall correctly." Sebastian felt enormously pleased with himself. Not only was he guiltless of having offended this man previously, he now had a bond to connect with him. Sebastian was not an approval seeker, and he normally detested the thought of ingratiating himself with someone who obviously didn't like him, but he felt obligated for poor Eva's sake. Besides, maybe the old man wasn't so bad after all. If he had

75

been a member of the Compass Society, he'd probably look down on some boring, know-nothing schlub trying to date his daughter, too. For a mad instant, Sebastian even considered revealing that he was a superhero.

"Well, you sound like you're very familiar with the Compass Society," Matthew replied flatly.

Evangeline went rigid. She stared across the small table at Sebastian, her eyes wide with alarm. She clenched her jaw and tried to warn him off by shaking her head, but he didn't notice.

"Of course! I have *Terra Incognita* journals going back ten years!"

"And what a coincidence that you remember me, of all people." Matthew's voice was sardonic, and he looked disapprovingly at his daughter. Eva wilted under his gaze.

"No, honestly!" Sebastian protested. "I remember particularly because the Cibola Expedition was in the same volume as Doc Strange's trip to Pellucidar. That was my favorite as a kid. I knew I recognized you, too, because I remember there was a photo of you in the cockpit of the *Subterrene.* I can't even imagine what that must have been like; to go places like that, to work with Rex Hazzard and Geo Templeton. Did you ever meet the Promethean?"

If anything, Matthew Garver looked more displeased that Sebastian's enthusiasm was sincere and not coached by his daughter. "It sounds like you think very highly of those adventurers... those *superheroes* like Strange and the Promethean." He pronounced the word 'superheroes' with unmistakable contempt.

76

Sebastian was baffled. "Well, I mean I don't know any of them personally or anything, but... yes, I guess I do."

Matthew regarded him with a sour face. Abruptly, he pushed himself away from the table and stood up. "I'm sure that says something about you, Mr. Pereira, although I'm not sure what. Evangeline, you'd better finish up so your friend can go home. I'm sure his parents want him back at a reasonable hour." With that curt dismissal, he walked away.

Evangeline slumped in her chair and pushed her plate forward, staring pleadingly across the table at Sebastian. He didn't know what else to do except finish his plate.

Once the front door closed behind them and they'd descended the steps, Sebastian erupted. "What the hell was all that?" He glared at Eva, who was holding her hand over her forehead.

"God, Sebastian. I'm so, so, so sorry. I should have said something to you, but..."

"I thought you were exaggerating, but you didn't tell me the half of it. What did I do wrong, huh?" More than indignation, he felt disgusted at himself for trying to be friendly to a man who obviously held him in contempt.

"He's really sensitive about the Compass Society and things like that. I never thought it would come up, otherwise I would have warned you."

Sebastian stormed off down the sidewalk, too angry to look back at her. "Please, he disliked me before he even heard my name!"

"Sebastian, hold on!" Her voice was quaking. She grabbed him and tried to drag him back.

77

He turned slowly and saw her eyes glistening with tears, and his heart overflowed with sympathy. Once again he noticed how warm her hands were.

"I'm sorry I put you through that," she said. "I knew he was going to be a jerk, but if I thought it was going to be that bad, I would never have asked you to come. Please believe me."

Sebastian laid his hand on her shoulder. "I do believe you. I'm sorry, Eva. I guess I screwed things up for you, huh? I didn't mean to."

"I know you didn't, Sebastian. Please don't be mad at me." She clamped both of her hands around his wrist and looked up at him beneath heavy eyelids. "Pittsburgh's been great, and school has been great, mostly because of you. I'd hate it if you didn't want to talk to me anymore. I'd understand completely, but I'd hate it."

"Hey," he said, and laid his palm on her cheek. "Don't worry about it, Eva."

"We're still friends then?"

"Yes. Absolutely we are."

She stood on her tiptoes and kissed his cheek. "I better get back inside," she whispered. "Call me when you get home?"

Sebastian was too stunned to do anything but nod stiffly. He wanted to kiss her back on the lips. He wanted to hold her close. But the moment passed. She pulled away and walked backwards toward her house, and he mentally cursed his cowardice.

"Bye!" she waved.

"Bye."

Thorpe Was Here

Did you ever see graffiti somewhere really ridiculous and wonder, 'How in the hell did they get up there?' You did if you lived in the Burgh.

THORPE WAS HERE. It was a triumphant proclamation and a defiant challenge that rang out in spraypaint from the tops of suspension bridges, the glass-walled penthouses in Commonwealth Tower, the peaks of barge cranes moored in the middle of the rivers, and even the top of the dome at Yellow Jackets arena. Many of the tags were so difficult and dangerous to access that the maintenance crews balked at painting them over, so they were left untouched for months or years. No eyes and no cameras had ever conclusively caught Thorpe in the act, but there was an urban legend that one night a cop saw him rappelling down the north tower of the Carnegie Bridge, 110 feet above the Mon. The cop got out of his car and ran down the maintenance access to catch him, but when he got to the bottom there was nothing but a dangling rope. When the baffled cop made it back to the deck, he found that Thorpe had been there, too, and left him a cheeky message on his rear windshield.

Thorpe was making all sorts of people who desperately needed to be taken seriously look ridiculous, and to them he was public enemy number one. But to the man on the street he was quickly morphing from a common vandal into a folk hero.

Eventually, Thorpe stopped tagging, but he was never caught and nobody ever figured out who he was. Nobody, that is, except for Torrent and X.

It was about ten days after the Grimalkin incident, which left me ambivalent about more than just the vigilante business. Mother Nature seemed to be having the same sort of mixed-feelings about the weather right about then, too, alternating between days of bitter cold and rain and warm, sunny days that foretold of spring. These warm stretches were a welcome reprieve from a too-long winter and they demanded activity outdoors, activity that did a lot to lift me from my funk. But the nice weather must have had the same sort of effects on the criminal element because there was a sudden rash of vandalism, muggings, and break-ins that called me to once again put on the mantle of Torrent.

Alex went back to patrolling with me regularly after I told him about what happened in Hazelwood. Once I overcame his skepticism, he was really excited about the whole affair - actually, thrilled might be a better word - and he cursed himself for not coming along that night. Not having come up with a better *nom de guerre*, he was still calling himself X, though he'd put a bit more creativity into his outfit. We went out every night that it wasn't bitter cold, and we found enough to keep us busy without having to go too far from home. We'd put the scare into some rock-throwing delinquents outside the Methodist church on Baum, and the night afterwards we'd chased off a couple of hoodlums breaking into cars down by the Quad at CMU. This night, the night we caught up with Pittsburgh's most notorious graffiti artist, we were hunting for muggers around the shops on Walnut Street.

That neighborhood is a classic "high-low" crime area. The crime rate is not what you'd consider epidemic (especially compared to some other parts of the city) and most of the incidents are non-violent, but it's still much higher here than in the other parts of Shadyside. For that I place the blame squarely on the Walnut Street Business Association, the block government for that neighborhood, for painting a big target on their back. Most of the storefronts have signs prohibiting their customers from carrying any sort of weapon. In fact, the prohibition is written into their bylaws. The WSBA didn't subscribe to any of the patrol services either, relying on their own "Prevention Force," which was perfectly toothless thanks to the unofficial prohibition on the use of force, even in self-defense. For example, a clerk at the the Antipodes Cafe, a snooty "exotic tea and coffee boutique", was actually fired for fighting off a robber last year. The Post-Gazette quoted the owner: "I won't condone the escalation of violence. That young man could have been seriously hurt or he could have seriously hurt the robber, and I don't want to live with that on my conscience. We have insurance. We don't need to do any of that.."

I can't say for sure which toxic philosophy produces that sort of mentality, but the WSBA is stewing in it. But hey, what do I know? They're still open for business, and people keep giving them money.

Anyway, there'd been at least one attempted robbery and one successfully completed in the past week, both times it was women who'd been walking home alone after a night of shopping and dining. The Pittsburgh PD showed their usual commitment to public safety by sending a couple of cops to sit in the car picking their noses during the daylight hours and go home at six o'clock. Needless to say, they didn't catch anyone.

Alex and I started patrolling around 8:30. We orbited the three-block area on our bikes, sticking to the dimly lit, tree-shaded side streets. Whenever we saw a woman walking alone or in a small group, one of us would ride a few blocks ahead on the look-out for predators while the other hung back behind them, waiting for the call on the walkie-talkie. We called this a deterrence patrol: if we saw anybody that looked shady, particularly if they were standing around in one spot or paying a little too much attention to the ladies, we'd roll up across the street from them and stare them down until they walked away. And they almost always did. Inevitably, a couple of them got belligerent and you'd hear some nasty remark about your mother or the way you're dressed (my goggles were a favorite), but we wouldn't say anything back, didn't escalate anything, just stared at them quietly until they lost their nerve and moved on.

I was on my way back to rendezvous with Alex after a successful stare-down when someone screamed in the far off blackness. I was about to thumb on the walkie-talkie and call it in when the speaker crackled and Alex's voice came through, tense and eager.

"I just heard a scream, maybe about a block from here. I'm heading north on Maryland Ave now. It might have come from around Summerlea Street."

"Copy that. I'm on my way, X" I said. I flipped the electric assist on my bike to pick up speed on the flat and raced to meet him there.

The screaming got louder as I barreled through the darkness and I could clearly hear a desperate cry for help. I could feel my heart pounding in my temples. I pedaled faster, so fast that my feet were falling off the pedals and I lost control of the damn bike; I nearly ended up going through the back windshield of a parked car. I throttled back the assist, but I was still zipping along and I had the momentum of the downslope so I got there at almost the same time Alex did, and we nearly T-boned in the intersection.

Alex skidded to a stop and leapt off his bike, his red scarf whipping back in the wind. He dashed down the street, screaming obscene threats. My eyes tracked his direction and I saw two men in half-silhouette man-handling a screaming woman. They were pulling hard on what must have been her purse, but the strap was caught, twisted around her captive arm, maybe.

"Stop! I can't let go!" she screamed again, and one of them screamed back, "Shut up, bitch!" There was a loud snap and the woman went back on her rear end, yelping. The two thugs took off in a sprint immediately. They knew X was close behind them.

I throttled up the power assist again and shot off after them. They were good runners - a lot faster than me - and sure-footed, but I was overtaking them quickly and so was X. Just as I passed Alex, I saw him out of the corner of my eye springing forward, his hands open, arms thrust in front of him to tackle the hindmost mugger. The muffled wet-meat-slapping-pavement sound and the groaning told me he connected, but I had to keep my attention on the lead thug who had the bag.

I beat him to the end of the block by a good twenty five feet, dismounted, and stood there blocking his path with my stun baton crackling. The little puke gaped at that. I mean you could really see the fear in his face. I thought for sure he was going to stop, but he didn't. Instead he stretched those long legs of his over a low stone retaining wall and made to cut across the tiny front yard of the last apartment building on the block. I lunged sideways, stretching out as far as I could with the shock stick, but the lucky bastard snuck by and I landed in the dirt, swearing.

He probably would've gotten away if it hadn't been for that motion sensor light that kicked on. It slowed him up a little bit, and it allowed me to see the spigot coming out of the wall of the house. I let my mind stretch out - yes, there it was. I could feel the water under pressure behind the ball valve. I concentrated on it, trying to push it open. The valve didn't budge.

But the pressure blew the loosened spigot right off the pipe-end! The spinning piece of cast iron rocketed into the creep's thigh just ahead of the spray of scalding water, and he fell sideways onto the pavement, flailing and whimpering.

I pushed myself up out of the dirt and trotted off after him. He'd gotten up too and was limping away, his grubby paws still clamped on that purse. I called after him.

"That was no coincidence, shitbird. Now give it up before I really hurt you."

He spun around, dug something out of his pocket and flicked his wrist at me. The tip of the switchblade glinted in the muted amber light of the street lamps. "We'll see who gets hurt!"

I pressed on the baton and smiled as miniature whipcracks of lightning lit up my face. I wanted him to know I was really looking forward to it.

Well, I never got the chance because in a minute he was down on the ground, screaming for mercy, and that little switchblade was kicked clear into the street. As quick as I blinked, somebody had run up behind him, put him in an armbar and planted his face on the pavement, and there that somebody was, still leaning on him.

"Give up?" the stranger whispered.

"Yes! Ow! Ow! Ow! Yes, I give up!"

The stranger released his lock on the thug and pulled him to his feet with one hand. With the other he picked up the purse. "Get lost, then."

I squinted at him. At first I thought it was X, but it wasn't, and then I thought it was one of the neighbors, but something didn't look quite right about him. He had eyeblack on - like the kind outfielders wear - but it covered the whole orbits of his eyes, and he had a black bandana tied around his head. A mane of long black hair curved down his forehead and over his brow, and it glistened with sweat. He was wearing open-fingered leather gloves and a tight black compression shirt that showed off his physique. He was taller than me by half a foot and built like a linebacker in the chest and shoulders, but like a sprinter from the waist down. His torso tapered to a narrow vee at the waist and his legs were long and lean. I assumed he had to be a vigilante like us.

"Thanks, pal," I said, and started to explain what happened. "This creep and his buddy stole that purse from a lady down the street, slapped her around a little bit, too." I extended my hand and introduced myself. "I'm Torrent."

He looked at me a moment, and I saw a thought come into his eye as the corner of his lip curled up in a smile. I knew right then I didn't like what he was thinking. "Torrent, huh?"

"Uh, yeah," I said, and let my hand drop. I eyed him warily. "If you don't want to hang around, I can take the bag back to her myself."

"Can you really?" He let out a short, deep laugh and took off running.

I swore, then doubled back to grab my bike. As I started pedaling after him, I called out his description to Alex on the walkie-talkie and told him to hurry, because the guy was moving fast. Incredibly, he was still out-pacing me on the straightaway, so I switched the bike to full power and gave my aching legs a rest. I gained on him.

And then he did exactly what you expected: he jinked down an alley and I went flying past him.

By the time I got the bike turned around, I caught a glimpse of him leaping straight up, an easy six-foot vertical. Dangling from one hand was the purse, while the other arm, outstretched, snagged the bottom rung of a retracted fire escape ladder. He swung his body around the bottom of the ladder in one smooth arc and came up the other side, upside down, like an Olympic gymnast on the uneven bars. He hooked his toes on an upper rung of the ladder and then flipped backwards, righting himself and continuing the climb up to the first platform of the fire escape. He laughed with manic joy as he scaled the building.

I just stared, slack-jawed.

The brakes of a bicycle squealed behind me.

"What the hell?" It was X. He was staring up at him, just like I was.

"That bastard is the second coming of Tarzan," I said.

Suddenly the jerk stuck his head out from behind the wrought iron ledge and taunted us. "Giving up already, tough guys? I'm just getting started!"

"Screw that guy," X barked. "What's he going to do, hide on the roof?"

Not a second later we saw him catapult himself from the ledge of the fire escape to the lower roof of the adjacent building, and then again to the next.

We followed him down the street, not by sight, but by his wild hoots of laughter. At the end of the block, he leaped from a low, gabled roof to a street lamp and then back down to street level. "Is this more fair for you?" he yelled.

"I'm going to break his face... if we ever catch him," Alex vowed between panting breaths. I wasn't so sure.

The street sloped sharply up a hill and then curved westward, running along the shoulder of an embankment. Beyond the guard rail yawned a gap of fifty or sixty feet, the bottom of which carried a spur of the railroad. A concrete road bridge spanned the gap, but it was a good six blocks away. Here there was only a narrow metal trestle, fenced off at both ends, carrying a gas main. You can already guess where we found our man.

"Let's see some hustle, mystery men!" he yelled as he catapulted himself over the chain-link and landed on the trestle with barely a wobble.

"No way," I said. My throat was tight and my stomach was already rolling just from watching him. He might as well have just ripped off the Crown Jewels; there was no way I was following him.

"Hurry, damn it!" X yelled.

"Don't be stupid! That's suicide!" I yelled back. He knew damn well I was afraid of heights. But X was already scrambling up the fence and muscling himself over.

When he landed, he pushed his face against the fence and yelled: "Stop being a pussy!"

It sounds ridiculous now, but at the time that was enough to settle the matter for me. I girded my loins and rushed the fence. The whole time I kept my eyes glued on the opposite embankment, thinking that if I just didn't look down, if I just didn't think about it, I could manage. The trestle was wide enough for two men bigger than me to cross, after all, and there was no more reason that I should lose my balance here than on the sidewalk. Those are the kind of lies I told myself as I put my weight on the first cross-beam, and then the wind hit me and I swayed like a Jenga tower after the third shot of whiskey. I leaned forward to rebalance myself, hyperventilating as I imagined all the ways my bones could rearrange themselves after a

drop of twenty feet onto talus. 'All the Burgh's surgeons and all the Burgh's men couldn't put Torrent back together again…'

I felt X's gloved hand land on my shoulder, anchoring me. "You're OK," he insisted. I was inclined to disagree.

He went off ahead of me. I tried to follow, but my feet might as well have been planted in concrete. It didn't seem to matter though, because our foe wasn't getting any farther. The fence at the other end was high and angled back over the trestle at the top. I didn't think this would have posed any obstacle to this guy, and it probably wouldn't have if it hadn't kept pulling loose from the posts and swinging back over the gap whenever he put his weight on it.

"Nowhere to run now, you son of a bitch!" X yelled into the wind.

"Don't be stupid! What are you going to do, fight him on the high wire?" I yelled, hoping to talk some sense into him before he got himself killed. I took a few unsteady steps toward him, but then a fresh gust of wind whipped down the ravine and knocked me off balance. I wobbled to the left, then lunged to the right, but I overcompensated and went tumbling. Everybody screamed, most of all me. At the same time as I slipped through the crossbars and my body rolled around the gas main, I saw the other guy drop from the sagging fence. I'm sure I felt bad for him, but as I was dangling there with just one arm bent around a rusty girder, I had enough to worry about. I tried to swing my legs up, but that just increased the pressure on my arm, and the pain was incredible. I felt my grip going numb from the lack of blood flow. I heard Alex

90

yelling to me, saw him crawling towards me out of the corner of my eye, but he was too far away. I knew I'd had it.

Then I felt a tug on my belt, heard a strained grunt as I felt myself rising. Suddenly I was high enough to wrap both legs around the girder and painfully swing myself back to the top of the trestle. I was spent both physically and psychologically, and I went limp. Then, looking down through that lattice of steel, I saw Tarzan Jr. himself swinging across the bottom of the trestle like it was an overgrown set of monkey bars, and the lady's purse was clamped between his teeth. Somehow, instead of plummeting to his doom, he had saved himself and then swung all the way back over to save me.

I watched slack-jawed as he brachiated back across the to the far end of the trestle and then pulled himself up. "On second thought," he called to us, "maybe you boys have had enough for one night! Here, catch!"

He lobbed the lady's purse at us, and X caught it between two hands. Then, one foot at a time, the stranger stepped onto a length of steel cable no wider than my thumb and tight-rope walked down it to the middle of the decrepit telephone pole that it anchored to the hillside. As he stepped onto the handhold, he gave us one more look and shouted, "It wasn't much of a challenge, but thanks for trying!" Then he scrambled down the pole, whooping noisily and declaring to all the world that "THORPE WAS HERE!"

That wasn't the last time we ran into him, and once we even got a good look at him from a picture Threads snapped. Alex recognized him right away - not somebody we knew personally, but somebody we'd all heard about. Somebody *you* heard about. What? You don't expect me to out him, do you? The statute of limitations hasn't run out yet on criminal trespass and defacement of public property, you know. All I'll say is that everything makes perfect sense: his peerless athleticism, the chase, and his chosen alias.

Not long after that night, people stopped seeing new Thorpe tags on the sides of buildings. Most people figured he'd been killed pulling one of his stunts. We knew better. Once in awhile we'd find some lowlife mugger knocked senseless with a *'THORPE WAS HERE'* index card on his chest, or scrawled on his forehead in permanent marker. See, it wasn't about the tagging any more than it was about a lady's purse: it was about the challenge. We just introduced him to a worthier kind.

Seduction of the Innocent

Sebastian gazed across the ring, an atoll of chairs and students spread out as wide as the little second-floor room in the St. Bonaventure schoolhouse would allow, studying the angelic face of Evangeline Garver. Her pink lips curled in a pensive moue and her eyes narrowed in concentration, her irises like tiny serpentine moons rising above the hills of her plump, freckled cheeks. She seemed not to notice his staring, seemed not to notice anything besides the spirited controversy in the ring, except once to irritatedly brush from her eyes a long coil of her red hair. She was totally absorbed in this boring, pretentious exchange of unsubstantiated assertions and jumbles of concepts only half-understood by their utterers, and he wondered why. A forlorn sigh left his lips and he slumped against the back of the plastic chair. He had come only at Evangeline's bidding; she was confident enough that he would at least be interested, if not engaged. "You have opinions," she had said. 'Yes, yes,' he wanted to say, but didn't, 'but none so puerile, and none on so tedious and unimportant a subject as metahuman rights.'

That cause had no ally in Sebastian Pereira, though he was himself (secretly) a metahuman. To him, even speaking the phrase was a sign of a careless mind easily provoked to reaction by shoddy logic and emotional hot buttons. He despised the movement rhetoric and the cavalcade of phonies that claimed to be speaking for him as they worked themselves into a lather over largely imaginary grievances. It was an obscenely disingenuous play for special privilege, seeking rights that nobody should have in the guise of demanding rights they already did have. In the Commonwealths, Talents had always been equal under the law; there was nothing going on that even superficially resembled the talent bondage of New England's National Program, yet these activists never stopped babbling about oppression and slavery.

A good example of this foolishness made the news last week, and the item had been broached already in this debate: one poor soul had been "oppressed" at the hands of a private businessman who refused him service at a bar. Sebastian assumed that everyone would've understood the owner's right to refuse whomever he wants for whatever reason he wants, even if they thought his reasons were bad. After all, wasn't that the same right a potential customer had? Not this fellow who is now agitating for laws to force, one imagines, everyone to be friends with everybody else. The old meta supremacists had blood on their hands, but at least they were honest.

But what Sebastian found most odious about the movement, even moreso than the assaults on free speech and free association, was the mendacious attempt to reframe seemingly every unusual occurrence and notable figure throughout human history as a talent in disguise. Mythological creatures, religious texts, folklore, even well-attested historical personages – no one and nothing were safe from this revisionism. Once, he facetiously argued to a meeting of the Talent Action Network that North America enjoyed its notably higher concentration of talents because Virginia Dare, first English colonist born here and who in legend transformed into a white doe, must have been a zoomorph. His sarcasm went undetected amongst the Tanners, who acclaimed his "bold" and "open-minded" analysis of history.

With a history of profitless interaction with these partisans under his belt, Sebastian had no intention of breaking his silence, though the temptation to rebut was maddening. He glanced down at sheet of yellow paper on his lap, a copy of a flyer that had been circulated at the start of this session. On it was a rank of shouting figures, all in silhouette, with angry fists raised above their heads. Some of the heads had zigzagging arrows radiating from them, a common graphic shorthand for psychic talents. A banner above and around it screamed: "Smash Mundanarchy! Direct Action against Bigotry, Intolerance, and Injustice!" Sebastian rolled his eyes, unwilling to read any more of it. He would try to tune them out and just keep on looking at Evangeline; he could do that all day.

But then C.J. Gravish, his pinched-nosed, oval-faced classmate who had been monopolizing the discussion, made a declaration so outlandish that it overwhelmed Sebastian's filters, and when he heard it he laughed like it was the punchline of a good joke. When Sebastian looked up again, the back-and-forth had ceased and a constellation of accusing eyes were drawn on him.

C.J. looked at Sebastian for a moment, pursed his lips and set his jaw like it was taking a great effort to master himself. "You disagree with my characterization of Magnetrix as a crusader for talent rights?" he said finally, his voice pitching higher as his pique increased.

"Well, I sort of assumed it was a joke that nobody else caught," Sebastian replied.

"You don't think much of her advocacy," C.J. continued. He eyed Sebastian ferociously. Clearly, he was caught up in the rush of the argument and was at the stage where no point of disagreement, no matter how trivial, would be left unshredded, and he was trying to draw Sebastian out for a decisive blow. C.J. fancied himself a master of rhetoric, and although Sebastian had other ideas about that, he knew him to have a sharp tongue and a biting wit. Sebastian had those qualities, too, so he knew that he would receive little sympathy from the crowd if he was, for once, the target of the exchange.

"It's her musical ability that I don't think much of. I never knew her to be a serious advocate for anything, except for herself," Sebastian replied.

"You really weren't aware of her past in the Global Parahuman Revolutionary Army?" C.J. scoffed.

"I am aware that she was kicked out, and that she was eager to turn state's evidence against her terrorist buddies in return for immunity. Probably because she only signed up on a lark." The statement provoked an isolated chuckle.

"That's certainly the perspective of a few of the GPRA... terrorists, as you identify them," C.J. allowed. "Probably you are ignorant of the strong themes of self-acceptance and social tolerance in her most recent album."

Sebastian smiled wryly. "I would plead ignorance of any but the basest and most lascivious themes in Magnetrix's music."

"And ignorant of Born Strange, the philanthropic organization she founded to fight intolerance and violence against talented youth," C.J. went on.

"Now that one I'm aware of," Sebastian said.

"But that doesn't meet your high standards for advocacy."

"To me, advocacy implies some level of sincerity. Magnetrix is a ruthless self-promoter who does what she thinks is most likely to attract attention. Positive attention, ideally, but when that can't be had, any attention will do. She wears causes like other people wear hats - or maybe more apropos for her, a pair of knickers, quickly soiled and kicked off at the first invitation."

That really kicked up laughter, and C.J. didn't appreciate it at all. Sebastian raised his voice above the commotion to tie up his point. "In short, Carl," he called C.J. by his full first name, which he had always done and had always chagrined him, "I think Magnetrix is a bad pop singer, and nothing more."

Sebastian leaned back in his chair and looked over at Evangeline for the first time since he'd unintentionally entered the discussion. She wore a little close-lipped smile, like she was trying to fight it. When his eyes met hers, she dropped them bashfully and scribbled something in her notebook.

"Alright then, Sebastian. Whom do you consider to be a worthy representative of the cause of metahuman rights?" C.J. asked.

Sebastian surreptitiously took a snapshot of the flyer with the miniature camera mounted on the nose of his eyeglasses and then made a show of crumbling it up and pitching it in a garbage can. "Oh, I don't know, really. I don't believe in metahuman rights," he replied casually.

You could hear a pin drop.

Sebastian was eager to disengage himself from the argument and was busy packing his backpack, so it took him a moment to notice the uneasy quiet. When he raised his eyes, the first face he saw was Evangeline's. She looked at him numb and disbelieving, as if he'd said he hated cats or called her a whore.

"Well, uh, what I mean is…" he stammered.

"You *don't* believe talents have *rights*?" gasped some outraged girl on the other side of the room.

"No…"

"Cabotist!" someone else shouted.

"Of all the repugnant, reprehensible beliefs…" C.J. Gravish started, but his tone was out of phase with his expression, for he was nearly smiling.

"I mean there's no such thing!" Sebastian shouted as he stood up, slinging his backpack over one shoulder. "I mean you can't just go around inventing rights and gifting them to one group or another. There are only natural rights, the same we all have, no more and no less. Now… that's all I can take of this stupidity for the day. Feel free to keep on badmouthing me after I leave, though."

Only a few minutes later, Evangeline caught up with Sebastian.

"For a while, I thought you weren't going to say anything at all," she said softly.

He shot her a cross look. "I hope you see now why I don't bother. I told you that Politics Roundtable was just a clique of self-righteous posers."

"I don't remember you saying that before now," she said.

"I guess I forgot to tell you. Sorry. They're a bunch of emotion-driven wimps and they wear their causes just like Magnetrix. Come on, you don't think Carl is a talent, do you?"

Evangeline seemed to shrink back. "I don't think you have to be metahuman to have a sincere opinion on the matter," she said in a small voice.

"No," Sebastian agreed, "but with most of them it's phony outrage." His words were angry, but his tone was matter-of-fact. The subject wasn't all that important to him, and it was only Evangeline's reaction that had left him flat-footed. She was the only one there whose opinion of him he really cared about, and she was still talking to him. Of course Evangeline would understand him.

"So, when you say you don't believe in metahuman rights..." she probed.

Sebastian slumped visibly. "I meant exactly what I said. You know, I was just thinking - literally, just now - that you, out of all people, would understand what I am saying and not try to figure me for a neanderthal."

"No, I get it, I do! Natural rights," Evangeline said. "But what about when they're dealing with entrenched discrimination? They're at a disadvantage then; it's not a fair situation. Isn't it OK to try and correct that?"

"Speak precisely, please."

"What?"

"You don't really mean 'try to correct that.' What you really mean is 'have the government coerce people into acting the way you want them to.' And the answer is always no. No, it's not OK to do that."

Evangeline was about to reply when the heft of his statement hit her, right between the eyes, as you might say. She opened her eyes wide and her mouth hung open, speechless.

"OK," she said after a little while, "but what about the talents that get beaten up, or worse?"

"Or enslaved, like in New England? Of course that's evil, but we don't live in New England."

"It's not just in New England. Meta kids get assaulted all the time in Pennsylvania."

"I don't think that's true, at least not that it happens any more often than normal kids getting assaulted," he said.

"Well why not?"

"It just sounds unreasonable. Don't you think? I mean, if you have actual superpowers, I'm sure you can handle yourself," Sebastian replied.

"But not every talent has violent abilities!" Evangeline insisted.

"So what, jocks are going around beating up spoon-benders for fun? How would they even know? And even if they did, is that really any worse than them picking on the kids with the overbites and the orthopedic shoes?" He arched his eyebrow at her. "Or the girls whose skirts are covered in cat hair?"

"I think it is worse," she muttered.

"OK, well I don't," he said, and stopped short of saying, 'and you're wrong.' "It's the same problem with a different face: some people are jerks and they get off on hurting other people. It doesn't pay to overreact to it or to try to reengineer society to get it to go away. It's never going away. We live in a fallen world."

"So we just have to accept injustices? Is that what you mean?" Evangeline asked testily.

"Not accept them, no. But understand that they're not going away just because--"

"Because that's just nihilism!" she interrupted him.

"It's not nihilism!" he protested. "Look, there's a right way and a wrong way to deal with problems. Two wrongs don't make a right and all that. And all of the 'solutions' ginned up by the professionally sanctimonious pimps in the 'metahuman rights' lobby aren't just wrong, they're stupid. God hands them extraordinary abilities and they act like it's a burden. Pity me, I have superpowers!"

"It's probably a lot more difficult for them than you'd think, Sebastian," Evangeline said.

The taut muscles of his jawline rippled with tension as clenched them, but he said nothing.

"Anyway, I should get going to work," she said, turning away.

"Hey," he grabbed her by the arm and his voice softened. "What time is that thing tomorrow?"

She looked back at him sadly, then flicked her eyes away. "Um, what thing?"

"Tomorrow's Wednesday. That thing you said you wanted me to accompany you to. You never said what it was."

"Oh, yeah. Well, don't worry about it. Something else came up. It, uh, probably wasn't a good idea anyway," she said, shaking her head.

"Well hold on now," Sebastian began, but lost the words as the disappointment welled up in his chest. "Is this because of what I just said? Are you mad at me?"

"Have a good night, Sebastian," she said, unable to keep her own twinge of anger and disappointment out of her voice.

He laughed mirthlessly, incredulously. "So because I don't share every opinion with you, I'm not good enough to bring along? Fine by me, Eva. I'm not a three-ring circus for your emotions," he yelled after her, and then went his own way home.

That afternoon, Sebastian went directly home and tried to nap. He had no energy or enthusiasm for anything else after his altercation with Evangeline. Yet he found himself too bothered by it to get any sleep, either, and so he laid on his back and stared up at the ceiling, watching the light dim through the filter of his curtains as the sun westered and sank. On a whim, he decided to read the flyer that Carl had distributed at the beginning of the roundtable, the one he'd taken a snapshot of before theatrically tossing it in the trash. He sneered at the oh-so-clever and contemptuous *mundanarchy* neologism and its unoriginality. The shadowy figures and clenched fists, the ill-defined but ominous phrases like *direct action* and *resistance:* it was the usual radical boilerplate, and he wondered if all such organizations used the same printers, maybe even got a bulk discount. Then he saw clearly for the first time that it was no mere piece of propaganda, but an invitation. It read:

Join TOGETHER, Talents and ungifted, a UNITED FRONT for positive CHANGE.

And it was followed by an address and a time: Birdie's Tavern, Rain Street, East Liberty. 9PM Tuesday

His curiosity was satisfied by a few minutes of research on the grid. Birdie's, it turned out, was known as a talent bar, the way some others were biker bars or swingers' bars. The place had a bad reputation, too; one might almost call it notorious. It was the sort of bar where people leave in ambulances fairly regularly, but the cops don't bother to show up. The owner had been a member of NEMESIS, the defunct metahuman supremacist/terrorist group, and had served time for some low-level felonies. Rumor had it he was a bagman for the GPRA.

'A recruitment drive?' he wondered. And for soldiers or patsies?

It took only a minute for Sebastian to decide he was going.

***

'This is not the sort of place I should be going alone,' thought Sebastian, even as he took hold of the old brass latch to the front door of Birdie's Tavern. He had squared off against a couple of talents before in his short career, but never had he gone out

103

expecting to be literally surrounded by a hostile crowd of them. And they would be hostile, potentially, even if they didn't know his low opinion of super-powered radicals or the GPRA, even if they didn't know what he was really there for. And did Sebastian know what he was really there for? He was there to find out who was recruiting and for what, but beyond that, it was hard to figure out what his options were.

He'd gone as Torrent, pulled his masked hood down over his nose and clamped it on his face with his blue-tinted goggles. Nobody noticed because he didn't look out of place; there were a dozen other people with masks on in there, mostly domino masks or bandanas with eyeholes, but a few were of more elaborate composition. It was a throwback to the 1940s and '50s when masks and capes were the height of fashion, the same way everyone used to wear wigs and top hats. Except these were the hard times versions of those glamorous accessories, adopted by workaday outcasts to identify themselves as part of a scene, or an expedient for lowlifes to confuse witnesses and CCTV cameras. By association, Torrent felt vaguely ashamed of his own appearance.

There was a bouncer perched on a stool by the door, fat and burly in a tight black T-shirt, hairless but for a neckbeard, and his big arms were covered with tattoos. The bouncer nodded at Torrent but didn't ask for proof of age - luckily, for he hadn't even thought of that. Now, Sebastian had bought a gun before with his own money, and four weeks out of the year he bivouacked with his dad's company in the militia; and he could have walked into any pharmacy and put down $10 for an ounce of dope, and gotten it, too, if the pharmacist wasn't all that conscientious, but when it came to booze, the state of Pennsylvania was more reticent. Anywhere else in the Commonwealths, hell, in most of the rest of the continent, the legal drinking age was 16, but here in Pennsylvania it was 18, and he was more than a year shy of that magical age. It was an amusing thing to scruple over considering the prevalence of alcoholism in the state. Nevermind! Birdie's was *not* the kind of bar that carded customers.

The air was dimly lit and smoky and the floor was dotted with stained wooden chairs and cheaper particle board tables; Torrent guessed that they got broken regularly. There were high brass stools at the bar, behind which was the obligatory mirror, a trick to make you feel less claustrophobic, though the interior was not particularly cramped. Torrent found a gap at the bar and slid in sideways, asked the prune-faced bartender what was on tap. She directed his attention to the tap handles with an unfriendly toss of her head and waited for him to decide.

"Uh, Yuengling, please," he said, not thrilled with his options, and slid a couple of dollars across the wet countertop. He glanced up at the clock on the wall as she returned and took the fee.

"I guess since I ain't never seen you before that you're here for the meeting," she said.

Torrent nodded. "I am, indeed."

She tossed her head again and her stringy, gray-brown ponytail bounced. "Back room," she said.

"Thanks, and keep it," he said. He took a swig and walked over to the swinging door at the end of the bar. Someone walking fast across the room with his eyes down and the collar of his winter coat pulled up nearly collided with him. He looked up for a moment, wide-eyed, and muttered an apology. Instinctively, Torrent looked away because he recognized the round face and the pinched nose and the swoop of black hair pasted with sweat to the forehead: it was C.J. Gravish.

C.J. slipped through the doorway, fortunately not recognizing him. Torrent was surprised; true, Carl had passed out the flyers, but Sebastian never, ever imagined that he would come here himself.

There were fewer people in the back room, only four of them besides Torrent and a man and a woman standing on a raised platform facing the crowd that he pegged for the meeting's organizers. He thought the girl, who looked about his age, was exceptionally pretty in a down-home, back-country sort of way, with little imperfections that worked to highlight her natural attractiveness. She had a clear complexion and wore no make-up except for indigo eye shadow, and the straight, full-bodied mane that tumbled down past her shoulders was glossy black. She had the farmer's daughter's build, slender but strong, with athletic curves accented by her tight denim jeans and tapered jacket. The man beside her looked older, but maybe only on account of the field of rough stubble on his blocky jaw. What little hair he had was done up in a faux-hawk, but the rest of his pate was shaved by choice, not to cover up early baldness like the fat bouncer. He stood with his booted feet planted shoulder-width apart, his arms crossed, flexing his thickly muscled forearms. Torrent at first assumed they were a couple, but soon noticed a distinctive family resemblance in their eyes and facial structure, and he wondered if they were brother and sister.

The pair waited five minutes past 9 to get started, apparently hoping in vain more people would show up.

"Lock the door!" the faux-hawk's voice suddenly boomed. Torrent tried to keep himself from jumping in surprise. Someone crossed behind him and slammed the bolt on an old slide lock, and Torrent tried to suppress the feeling that he'd made a big mistake in coming here.

"I hate being interrupted," he continued with a Kanawha mountain twang. "If they can't show up on time, we don't want 'em anyway." There were a few growls of agreement.

Sebastian sipped his beer and examined the weight and thickness of the glass, just in case.

The girl stepped forward and smiled coyly, showing off a dimple beneath her strong, high cheekbones. "At least there's some men with balls in this city," she said to a chorus of affirmative grunts.

"Let's get down to business," she said, slipping out of her jacket and tossing it over an old crate. Torrent sucked in a breath of air between his teeth and stared. Underneath she had on a tight, electric blue compression top that left her flat abdomen bare. Around her navel were traceries of softly glowing filaments, winding their way up her body until they disappeared under the shirt and reappeared again on her shoulders and the sides of her neck, curling up to her chin. The network of sub-dermal fiber optic thread and body heat-powered diodes traced out an elaborate scene of twisting ivy and blooming flowers. He always thought tattoos, especially on women, looked trashy, but the delicate lines and diffuse, ethereal glow of her electoos were enticingly otherworldly, far classier and elegant than could be scrawled out in ink.

"I'm Cascade, and this is my brother, Scald. We're with the Paras. And we didn't come here to waste time sweet-talking and cajoling you. You know what we want, and I guess if you're here then you want the same things." She started counting off on her fingertips: "First, we want our freedom; freedom to live as we are and the freedom to remake the world as it should be. Two, we want our rightful due, all the good things that have been denied us by a hateful and greedy system of oppression. Three, we want... vengeance. Vengeance against every person and every institution who wronged one of us, or sat by, silent, while one of us was wronged. And that means making life uncomfortable for *a lot* of people."

'Finally, some honesty!' thought Torrent. Her list was terrible, just terrible, but it was a breath of fresh air compared to the meandering duplicity of C.J. Gravish's politics workshop. He immediately looked over at his classmate to study his reaction. He was nodding vigorously, almost vibrating with nervous enthusiasm. 'The little worm,' Sebastian thought, and he wondered if indeed Carl wasn't a talent, or at the very least a spoon-bender. How else could he be so sanguine about that "new world" that Cascade was talking about building, one where there wouldn't be

109

much place for soft, *ungifted* Carl Gravish. Was he so naive as to think her rhetoric was as empty as his own?

"I'll be honest with you: this job is hard. This job is dangerous. The pay sucks, and there are no vacation days or retirement plans, except maybe a prison cell or a shallow hole in the ground. But you don't join the GPRA for a comfortable living; you join the GPRA because it's the right thing to do. You join because it's your duty. You join because your brothers and sisters in New England are in bondage, because talents make up 5% of the population but 15% of the prisoners, because of the parents neutering their own children with *Psicloban*, because of the talent kid that was shot to death in Wheeling last week, with no charges filed. You do it because you know the incidence of talent expression has declined steadily over the last decade from all the poisons that government and industry have pumped into your air and water." Cascade paused, and then looked at each one of them in turn. "And you do it because you know the war is coming and that we're sure as hell going to be the ones to win it, and you don't want to be counted among the collaborators when it's all over."

'Hot damn, she's good,' Torrent thought, feeling a dark and brutal corner of his psyche stirring. He had to remind himself that her numbers were questionable and that the story about the kid in Wheeling was, at best, a half-truth to keep himself from agreeing. Her delivery was perfect, and she hit all the right emotional chords, including that final, supremely confident, with-us-or-against-us note.

"Where do we sign up?" a gruff voice shouted, followed by approving hoots.

"What do you think this is, the 4H?" Cascade laughed, and her tinkling laughter was intoxicating. "There's no sign-up. You join by doing. And we've got plenty for all of you to do."

"But you start at the bottom and work your way up," Scald barked. "We got to know how reliable you are."

While the other four men, Carl included, went forward to see what the GPRA asked of them, Torrent hung back, committing to memory whatever he could of their features and voices. He sipped his lager and strained his ears to hear what tasks Cascade and Scald had set out for them. Each was asked what their talent was; one of them said he could see in the dark, and another said something about always being able to find out where someone was. He was especially interested to hear what Carl's answer was and to gauge their reaction, but he couldn't hear and Scald's back was turned. Torrent lay his glass down and stepped forward, ready to put himself in the thick of it.

He was stopped by a slender hand pressed against his chest. "Now, you look like the sort of man who's already gotten his hands dirty. Am I right?" Cascade said, smiling up at him.

Torrent smiled back. "Do I have that look about me?"

"What I mean is, your outfit isn't just thrown together. You've put some thought and maybe some money into it, like a man who knows he has to prepare himself for trouble," she said, fingering the

111

straps of his harness and glancing at the black nylon holster that held his retracted stun baton. "And when most people first put on a mask, they can't figure out how to keep it covering their face without it getting in their eyes, but you seem to have figured that out."

"It did take some figuring," he admitted.

"So I'm right?"

"You are right, Cascade," he said.

"I knew I was." She cocked her head sideways and ran her fingers down his sleeve. "And what should I call you? Your war name, I mean."

"Torrent."

"Torrent? And what's your talent, Torrent?"

"Oh, I have a couple," he said. "What about you, Cascade? What do you do, besides giving good speeches and wrapping men around your little finger?"

Cascade let out a little laugh and might have even blushed, but it was hard for him to tell in the dark room and through the tint of his goggles. "Can't you guess from the name?" She leaned against him and turned sideways, gesturing to the half-empty mug of beer he'd put on the table. Quickly the frothy alcohol streamed up the sides of the glass in defiance of gravity and congealed into a spinning and flashing globule suspended in the air.

Torrent hummed and inclined his head. The floating glob suddenly shot up into the air and burst into a rain of ale. Cascade looked startled that it had been wrenched out of her psychic control.

"And I thought you'd have guessed mine," he said.

"Hydrokinesis," she said, quickly hiding her surprise. "And strong, too. I had a good grip on that, Torrent. And you said you had other talents?"

"I'll keep that to myself for now."

"Ooh, mysterious," she teased.

"Cautious."

"Prudent," she nodded. "It's not just your outfit. You *do* have that look about you. Confidence, determination. You're that way because you've actually measured yourself against people, gotten things done. Don't worry, I won't ask what just yet. But I know how it is to go off on your own. My brother and I freelanced for a little while before we enlisted."

"Enlisted?"

"In the Revolutionary Army, of course. It's a little joke we have. That's what you came here for, isn't it?"

"Maybe," he said. "You gave a lot of good reasons to do something, but not necessarily good ones to join the Paras. Maybe I end up in jail or a morgue anyway, but I don't want to get there because your folks got sloppy or stupid, understand?"

"Very prudent," she repeated. "Torrent, we're the real deal and deadly serious. We don't screw around in what we do."

"Or who you associate with?" he said.

"Exactly."

Torrent replied with one word: "Magnetrix."

Cascade winced. "Take a walk with me," she said. "Outside."

He watched her gesture to her brother that she was going out, and that everything was OK. She led him to a darkened exit and pushed the door open.

"Allow me," he said, and held the door for her. "After you."

"You're very courteous, also," Cascade said.

Torrent smiled. "Or maybe just prudent?"

Torrent scanned the narrow alley and Cascade kicked the door shut behind them. "See? Nobody waiting out here to clobber you and take your fancy goggles."

"You're wondering if they have something to do with my other talents," he said, with a sudden burst of intuition.

"Are you a shrewd guesser, or merely a mind reader?" Cascade asked wryly.

Torrent inclined his head significantly. He wanted to be careful to not reveal too much about himself, and to keep her off-guard, if only to make it harder for her and Scald (and whatever other allies might be lurking around) to close in on him. He allowed that he was doing a pretty fair job of it, too.

"It's uncommon for a person to have multiple talents," she said as she walked down the alley. "That's extremely valuable for our cause."

"Where are you taking me?" he asked.

"Away from the riff-raff," Cascade replied.

They debouched into an open space, or so it seemed for it was too dark to see much away from the dimming light by the exit. But the walls had receded and the fierce April wind whipped about them. They heard the moaning of leafless trees straining against the gusts, invisible somewhere behind them.

"What do you know about Magnetrix, Torrent?"

He shrugged. "Only what all the reporters said, and maybe a bit more that I surmised. I can't figure out why, if you're so deadly serious, you let such an obvious liability enlist." On that point he was genuinely curious, but it was also his way of deflecting any well-placed suspicion they might have of him.

"Good question," she said, bitterly. "And Scald and I asked the same thing. But we didn't have anything to do with it. If it had been up to us, or a lot of other people, it would never have happened. I'd have dumped that whore in a hole somewhere and forgotten about her."

"It sounds like maybe you had to work with her for a while," Torrent observed.

"Maybe I did, and maybe I didn't. But what I did and who I know isn't any business of an outsider," she said curtly.

"Right you are, but you're not allaying any of my concerns about joining with you."

"She was powerful, and maybe that was enough for some people. And she had a podium with her music, and people thought she would take our message mainstream and get us the manpower we need for what's coming. Whatever, they were wrong." And she added sinisterly, "those responsible learned their lesson. Trust me on that."

For a little while, neither spoke. Then, Torrent said: "I came here tonight for a reason. I want to test the waters, but only test them, now, until I'm satisfied that this organization can really get something done, something besides making a laughingstock of itself."

"I understand completely," Cascade said. "You have to prove yourself to us, and we have to prove ourselves to you. We're up to it."

Her teeth began to chatter. "Damn it, it's cold out here," she said, and threw herself up against Torrent, slipping her arms into the pockets of his hood. For an instant, Sebastian was stunned, but then he wrapped his arms around her back and started to rub his palms vigorously against her bare skin.

"Oh," she whispered, "you're not that cautious after all, Torrent." Cascade ground against him and leaned her forehead against his. "I like you. I like men who do instead of talk. I like men who are men."

With those words and her hot breath on his lips and her body pressed against him, Torrent had all but forgotten about the GPRA's revolting ideology, even the borderline psychopathy manifest in her speech. Did she really mean what she said, intend the things that she talked about? He told himself she didn't and couldn't. He leaned forward to kiss her; she pressed his head back and slipped her tongue between his lips, whimpering. In that hot, hormonal instant all of those considerations were worthless. She wanted him the way a woman wants a man, and she was ready, eager to take what she wanted. Like him, she did while others talked, and it didn't matter that what she did was bad. Boldness itself had to be respected. What could petulant, self-righteous posers like C.J. and Evangeline know about any of that? Cascade could be mastered, he decided, once she'd been pulled out of her circle of cretins. If it came to it, he could slap some sense into her, and she would be grateful for it.

116

But then again, he thought, as he crushed her body against his and her fingertips wended under his clothes and pressed into his skin, maybe she was right about some things, too.

She pulled back suddenly and, looking him in the eye, licked her lips. "OK," she said breathlessly, "Let's get your feet wet."

"What do you need me to do?" Torrent asked. And already he had forgotten that he wasn't supposed to do it.

* * *

Burleigh Multimedia was a small print-on-demand company that ran out of the basement of an office building in Bloomfield. They weren't a publisher with editors and marketers, they just printed things, pamphlets and small books, mostly, that people paid them to print, and they made no judgments about what it was they were printing. They stood behind only the quality of their binding and covers, not the content of their work - that was for someone else to worry about. And the GPRA was worrying, because one of Burleigh's customers was a local writer with an anti-talent bent whose inflammatory political commentaries and full-color charts of the metahuman conspiracies rolled off its presses before being distributed for free in newspaper boxes throughout the city. The circulation of these writings was enough to earn the author a living from advertisement fees, but by any reasoned assessment, his influence on the tenor of talent/mundane relationships was negligible. But that didn't matter to the Paras, nor did it matter that this was only a small fraction of the printer's output: Burleigh Multimedia had been warned, had refused to bend, and now was to be sent a message. Cascade told Torrent all of this, along with how this was the perfect mission for him. By bursting a few pipes in the building overnight, he could flood the basement and damage all their back stock and machinery. With some luck, they'd go out of business entirely. "Let's get your feet wet", she said, and she meant it literally.

It wasn't a big deal, actually. Petty and mean-spirited, but easy enough to pull off, with minimal exposure to danger and very little chance of getting caught. After all, pipes burst all the time on cold nights like this. At least until the Paras took credit for the attack, which they would of course, but it'd be hard to tie it back to him. And as far as criminal penalties went, he'd already done things as Torrent that would have left him open to worse punishments. There *was* a danger, of course. The place was probably monitored with cameras and he'd have to get close enough and linger around long enough for his hydrokinesis to do the job. He would show Cascade that he could be trusted to do a dirty job and do it right, and that he was willing to stick his neck out for the cause.

Torrent stared at the Burleigh Multimedia sign on the side of the building from the pedestrian bridge that spanned the street, fully prepared to walk across the empty road and give those pipes a piece of his mind, and he had no way to explain why. He had walked all the way over here from Birdie's never once thinking that he was actually going to do it, telling himself he was just putting on a show (even

118

though he'd come alone). Now that he was here, he had to convince himself not to do it. If he did it, some ruined printers and reams of paper would be a small price to pay to get him into the bowels of the GPRA in Pittsburgh, where he could stop whatever serious crimes they were planning. Besides, this writer was a dick - Cascade had showed Torrent a pamphlet, and it was full of Unionist propaganda - and so was Burleigh for printing his garbage. They deserved it.

"Now you're thinking like a cop," he muttered to himself, bristling with self-loathing. But it was worse than just that. Those *were* just excuses, in the literal sense. The real reason he was actually considering doing this was because he didn't want to look like a chump in Cascade's eyes.

What a load of crap.

What would his big brother Rob have said if he saw him now? What would Alex say once he told him? No, Alex could never hear about this, Sebastian quickly decided. No one could.

Torrent turned around and started the long walk back home. His thoughts repeatedly turned back to his contempt for his classmate, C.J. Gravish, and his laughable naiveté, which didn't seem so laughable now that he'd nearly been snared by it himself. Whatever C.J.'s motivations were, at least there was the possibility that he actually believed in his cause, whereas Sebastian was ready to abandon both good sense and principle for the sake of a hard-on. That was a tough thought to sleep on.

The next day at school, Sebastian didn't talk to Eva. He had been humbled enough by his previous night's misadventure that he was ready to apologize for his surliness and smooth things over, but he never got the chance. She didn't meet up with him on the morning walk; he didn't see her at all until around noon, and then she went home without eating lunch. But all day he wondered what C.J. might have gotten himself mixed up in last night.

C.J. stayed very late that day, until nearly three o'clock. Curious, Sebastian hung around too and kept an eye on him, but never picked up any clue as to what assignment they'd given him. If C.J. had a guilty conscience about anything he did last night, or had any butterflies about anything he was supposed to do today, then he hid them well. Sebastian debated confronting him directly, or tailing him home, but ultimately decided not to risk exposing his alter ego by doing so. His brother's keeper he might well be, but his responsibility for Carl could only go so far. He wouldn't leave him entirely without advice, however.

When C.J. opened his locker to get his coat at the end of the day, a folded-up piece of paper fell out of the door with a handwritten note.

"Don't get involved. It isn't 4H, after all. - Someone Who Knows"

He jumped up and quickly crumbled up the paper as another locker door slammed behind him. He turned around, his face white.

"G'night, Carl," Sebastian said. He walked past him without sparing a glance.

"Oh, uh… yup. Good night."

***

Sebastian went right home that Wednesday. He thought about calling Eva, mentally rehearsed their

120

conversation, but he couldn't pull the trigger. Instead, he spent two hours trawling her YOrbit profile and the personal site with her poetry and short stories, all the contact info she'd shared with him when they bumped mobis the first day they met. It was the first that he'd spent any length of time going over it, and the more he read - her status updates, her random thoughts, her lonesome verse - the more his anger and hurt over their broken date subsided. His eyes tracked the cursor down to her universal contact line, finally ready to give her a call.

Then he noticed something he never expected. It was a link to a profile at another social network: 'MetaFriends - the Grid's best place for Talents to network anonymously.'

"TheUnprisonedFlame," he read the profile headline out loud, his eyebrows arching. "A 15-year-old female Thermokinetic."

Miasma

"I must have missed something," said Sebastian Pereira as he tightened the strap of his goggles and tugged his mask into place. The pair of vigilantes were standing in sparse woodland alongside the railroad tracks, beneath a deep dip in the land that hid the lights of Pittsburgh and left them in deepening shadow beneath the vernal stars. Sebastian, now in the guise of Torrent, continued: "I thought you said he had chemical burns?"

Alex Shepherd, his mouth shrouded beneath a red scarf - the disguise of the hero called The Mysterious X - nodded his head as he replied. "All over his chest and arms. He was treated at the decon facility at the Pitt medical campus."

"But they didn't find any trace of chemicals?" asked Torrent.

"Well, that's what they said. The paper said they tested the clothes and had some kind of chemical sensor sniff the air and they both turned up nothing. But that can't be true now, can it?"

"Unless the guy was a nutcase and he burned himself a long time before then."

"How does that explain the paramedic who passed out from the fumes?"

"Mass hysteria?" suggested Torrent.

"I thought you didn't believe in mass hysteria?"

Torrent grinned. "I don't."

"This is as blatant a cover-up as any we've seen. Nobody wants to touch the case; they've been passing the buck like a hot potato for two days. The fire marshal said his investigation is over because there were no chemicals; the city cops said they had no jurisdiction and it was up to the railroad security; the Pinkertons said the hobo couldn't have been riding one of the C&K trains and there were no chemicals on the trains anyway, so it's not their problem. Not one of them even interviewed the guy! Somebody, probably all of them, knows what really happened, but they're sweeping it under the rug."

Torrent couldn't find much room for disagreement with that assessment. "It *is* weird," he said. "But it sounds like one of those random, one-off events that my uncle writes about. Like a rain of frogs: it'll never happen again, and I don't think we'll find any clues." Paul Pereira, or "your crazy Uncle Paul" as Sebastian's father usually referred to him, was a freelance journalist who found his niche reporting on forteana and other tales of the bizarre and seemingly inexplicable. His wire stories were circulated by about two dozen major outlets and his online journal, *The Magic Casement*, was a popular resource for enthusiasts of the weird. Though a black sheep in his family, Uncle Paul was, in some ways, an inspiration for Sebastian.

The Mysterious X threw up his hands exasperatedly. "What are you talking about? Your uncle *did* write about this! The Tribune only mentioned it in passing, but your uncle was all over it. And I already said that this is the second time this week that a transient reported exposure to chemicals. How do you not know any of this? I thought you read his blog every day?"

Torrent shrugged. "I've had other things on my mind lately. Do you know what MetaFriends is?"

"Nope," said X.

"It's a social network for talents," Torrent explained. "It allows anonymous profiles for people who, for whatever reason, don't want to out themselves."

"And? You may recall that I don't have the crutch of superpowers."

Sebastian rolled his eyes under his goggles. He felt sure that Alex was the only vigilante who ever condescended about not being a talent. "Suppose someone had an anonymous profile - and I mean it didn't have their real name or picture or any sort of obviously identifying information, but they shared it with you. I mean, they shared it with you in person…"

"By bumping mobis?" X interrupted.

"Yes, exactly," Torrent replied. "Do you think it was something that person would do intentionally, like they wanted to discreetly let you in on their secret, or that it was an accident?"

X let out a low whistle as he considered the question. "I have to believe it was a major screw-up. If you want someone to know something like that, you tell them face to face, you don't give away the keys to the house, so to speak."

Sebastian thought about it, absently chewing his thumbnail. He had come to more or less the same conclusion as Alex. He'd been struggling over how to approach Evangeline ever since he'd discovered that she'd shared her MetaFriends profile link with him when they exchanged contact info. He couldn't decide how to respond to it: if he told her about it and she hadn't intended to share it with him, she would probably panic, and their relationship was already strained. On the other hand, if she had intended to share it with him and he just ignored it, how would that make her feel?

"So who was it? I know you're not dumb enough to make that mistake, and you wouldn't be asking that question if you had."

The question broke Sebastian out of his reverie. He looked across at Alex, uncertain how, or if, he should answer. Even if Eva had shared the profile intentionally with him, she definitely hadn't shared it with Alex. It wasn't his place to spill her secret.

"Just somebody I met, nobody you know," he answered.

"My ass," X replied immediately. "Since you're making me guess, I'm going to say it's Eva, and that's why you've been avoiding her at school."

"I haven't been avoiding her, she's been avoiding me." Torrent replied through nearly clenched teeth.

"So it's her then? Don't worry, you know I won't say anything about it. It's none of my business," X said. "I don't see what the problem is, though."

"I'll hold you to that," Torrent replied, but he knew Alex could be trusted. "Anyway, she thinks I hate metas."

"Why?"

Sebastian explained about last week's politics workshop and his own poorly received opinion about "metahuman rights", Magnetrix, and the Global Parahuman Revolutionary Army. "She seemed determined to misunderstand me," Sebastian finished.

No doubt Eva took it personally, especially since she had no clue that he was, himself, a talent; that explained why her reaction was so overwrought, so uncharacteristically Eva.

"Well, she's a chick." The Mysterious X shrugged. "You have to expect that kind of reaction."

"I want to put her at ease, but I don't want to tell her about me. Not yet."

"Definitely not!" X said. "We don't know her well enough to tell her about this."

"She probably wouldn't approve, anyway," Torrent offered.

"You never know. She might want to put on a costume." X paused thoughtfully and looked at Torrent. "She might already have a costume."

Torrent snorted at the suggestion and let the subject drop. On they marched in quiet beneath the swaying pines, following the railroad spur into the deeper darkness of the cleft called Panther Hollow and their eventual destination in the scattered hobo encampments of the Blight.

"Watch out, there's something in the path," said X, noticing something in the red light of his headlamp.

"I see it," remarked Torrent. The obstruction was a sheet of metal tied to two slanting wooden railroad ties sunk into the rock ballast of the railbed. "There's writing on it."

"More urban art," X quipped.

"No. Hoboglyphs," said Torrent. He switched his own headlamp from the red beam to the white and studied it. "It says: Do not Enter, essentially. There's a glyph for a safe campground and it's been crossed out," Torrent explained.

"You're bullshitting me. You can read 'hoboglyphs' now? Any pretty young girls ask you to tutor them in that?"

Torrent looked up into the red light of Alex's headlamp, smirking. "Not as of yet. But that's what it says." He stood up, spun around and searched the embankment. The light illuminated a little hollow, maybe only five or six feet wide, but deep enough that they couldn't see the end of it.

"I'm guessing there was a little camp spot back there. The arrow on the marker pointed this way."

"That sounds promising," X said. "We should go check it out. But I wonder how long it's been abandoned. The paint looks fresh."

Torrent kneeled and tapped a button on the side of his goggles, the wireless link to his mobi. "We might be able to get a firm date. Most transients travel with some sort of electronics today, and they also use GPS tags to back up the glyphs. There's a Geocaching node I visit that has a listing."

"It's encouraging that even penniless drifters have mobis nowadays," X said.

"The nice thing about the site, besides the timestamp, is that there's usually some longer commentary about the markers. Oh, here we go," Sebastian said as text scrolled past his eye on the inner surface of his goggles. He read it aloud: "Crazy motherfucker dressed like a bird stormed in on us, ranting and raving. 'Better run, better run!' Awful reek, worse than sewage, burned my eyes like crazy."

127

"Seriously?" Alex asked. "And you said we wouldn't find anything. When did this happen?"

"Three days ago. Gee, you'd think the cops and the Pinks would've picked up on a little tidbit like this, wouldn't you? Nice detective work, gents," Torrent remarked sarcastically.

"Not everybody can sit around school all day, accumulating useless knowledge from obscure Grid nodes," X needled him.

Torrent stood up, unholstered his stun baton. "What are you snarking about? It came in handy, didn't it?" He cocked his head toward the abandoned camp site. "Want to check this out?"

X held out his hand graciously. "After you."

If the two vigilantes actually expected to find a demented criminal in a bird costume, they were disappointed. There was little to be seen but a few benches made of logs and sheets of metal propped on cinder blocks, a tarp half-buried in deadfall and dirt, and a lot of litter. An old rusted steel drum showed evidence of fire, but the ash inside was cold and wet, and it hadn't rained since last week. If the fellow who posted the warning had actually set up camp there, either he returned later to collect his belongings or someone else had. Torrent wondered aloud if this might have been done to cover up evidence of a chemical attack.

"Well, there's nothing here now," X said. He had a thoughtful look about him and soon gave voice to those thoughts. "I wonder what that 'dressed like a bird' stuff was about. There's a lot of weirdos in the city, but I think it's too big a coincidence for this not to be connected with the chemical attack. Assuming it's the same guy, what does the costume tell us? A bird mask doesn't really look like a gas mask."

"No," Torrent agreed. "It doesn't."

"Did the hobo say how he was dressed like a bird?"

"Nope, only what I read to you and nothing more. He could've had feathers on his arms for all we know. Maybe he's one of us, only a flashier dresser."

"And a lunatic," X added.

"You know, you wondered about a gas mask, but the chemical could be mainly liquid or even a powder," Torrent mused. "I kind of hope that's the case, or that we don't run into this guy tonight at all. I sure as hell didn't bring a gas mask."

The Mysterious X hummed and unslung his pack. He pulled out something bulky, a vinyl sack closed with a drawstring. Out of this he retrieved a big bug-eyed mask with a large canister hanging down from where the mouth should be. "Well, what do you know. I did."

"Semper paratus!" said Torrent, laughing. "That thing's a relic."

"Pre-Pan American War. The guy at the surplus store said it was the 1965 model. But gas masks don't change much, plus it's made in Kalamazoo. If anybody knows about gassing people, it's the Union of the Great Lakes."

"How do you know it still works?"

"I bought a new filter for it, but..." X shrugged his broad shoulders. "I don't."

Their patrol continued into the Blight and to the margins of the switching yard and then they turned around, ready to call it a night. They hadn't seen a soul, nor any more clues to the mystery. But then, as they approached Panther Hollow from the south, just north of the highway overpass, they both noted a peculiar scent. At first it was faint and only a little unpleasant, like a whiff of old mothballs, but then a strong breeze funneled down the hollow, and the odor was noxious.

X rubbed his watering eyes with his fists and turned his head athwart the breeze. "Phew! What is that?"

Torrent gagged and spat and cupped his hands over his nose and mouth. The acrid, chemical odor burned the back of his throat and stung his nostrils until they swelled almost shut. "I think," he rasped, "you'd better put that mask on."

While Alex stopped to put on the mask, Sebastian tried to discover the source of the stink. It was obviously coming from the north, the direction they were now headed and the direction they had originally come from, but he couldn't see anything in the distance. Wherever and whatever it came from, the strong smell was abating, and he was thankful for it. When the scent faded completely, he breathed deeply to clear his nose and lungs. He tapped Alex on the shoulder.

"It's gone."

"That's nice." Alex's voice was muffled and distant-sounding through the mask. He still fumbled with the straps. "But I'm leaving the damn thing on, now."

The pair scuttled off the railroad tracks and sought cover in the low brush that lined the margin of the railbed.

"Take the lead," said X.

"What? You have the mask!"

"I can't see worth a damn in this thing!"

Torrent groaned and crept ahead. His head bobbed continually, first surveying the ground in the red light of his headlamp, carefully choosing his footing to minimize the noise of his steps, then peering straight ahead, looking for movement. 'This is nothing. A leaking gas truck on the highway or a backed up culvert,' he told himself.

Torrent was not really convinced there was a psychopathic gasser at all. It was easy to imagine how a leaking train car, a coincidental encounter with a nut in a bird costume, and ample panic could precipitate such a confabulation. The explanation for all this, if they ever found it, was bound to be much less interesting than Alex imagined. At least, this is what Sebastian told himself he believed, because he did not relish the thought of facing such a villain if he existed. He wasn't prepared for it, and, arguably functional gas mask aside, neither was his partner. Another stiff breeze rushed down the hollow, carrying only the faintest trace of that toxic smell. It was encouraging.

Then he heard a muffled whimpering and a burst of short, ragged coughs directly ahead of him, and that encouragement evaporated.

Torrent signaled to X, who nodded. He had heard it, too.

Torrent unholstered his shock stick. "We'll go together," he whispered. "I'll be your eyes until I get gassed, then..." But the nervous flopping in his stomach belied his smirk and joking demeanor.

131

"Let's do it!" X said. He sprang up with one of his lead-weighted batons in his fist. X toggled his headlamp to the brightest setting, valuing range and clarity of vision over escaping notice, but Torrent left the red-filtered nightlamp on. They moved quickly, each searching ahead and to the side for the source of the sounds.

"Over there!" X cried. The beam of his headlamp illuminated the foot of the embankment about ten yards away where two human forms, gagged and hog-tied, wriggled helplessly in the mud. The pair of vigilantes ran toward them at once.

X stopped at the nearest one. It was a man, his skin pale and clammy, in an coat with a huge, wet stain that reeked of the same noxious, burning odor they'd smelled before. X pulled the gag out of his mouth, and with it came a pool of chunky vomit. X held his jaw open and swept the inside of his mouth with his fingers to clear the airway. The man's eyeballs bulged from the force of his hacking, but he was breathing.

Behind him now, knife in hand, X tried to reassure him as he worked to cut through the rope that bound his limbs. "Take a deep breath now. I'll have you loose in a minute." But the victim thrashed like a pinned beast and screamed.

X rolled him over and clamped his hand down forcefully over his mouth, lest their attacker still linger in the area and be alerted. "Calm down," he hissed.

With hysterical strength the man snapped the few frayed strands of nylon that still bound his wrists and clobbered Alex with the side of his fist.

X scrabbled backwards and roared with indignation. "You jackass! I'm trying to help you!"

The other man didn't care; he only wanted to get away. He aimed frantic, but clumsy blows at X and even a few at himself, raving and screaming the whole time. When X put some distance between them, the guy bolted.

The rapid crunch of boots on rocks sounded behind him. X turned too late.

Torrent had just finished sawing through the rope that bound the wrists of the other captive when he glimpsed the huge, leering menace that suddenly materialized in the sweep of X's headlamp. Here was the bird-man; no colorful popinjay, but the corpse-fattened crow mask of the medieval plague doctor.

Torrent watched it as if in slow motion. Wide, lidless eyes shone like mirrors. A long beak, curving like a scimitar, seemed to open hungrily, a trick of the light as the head swiveled with the body, a heavy wooden pole sweeping out that same arc until it crashed into and bounced off of X's head. X went down without a sound, and the headlamp went spinning off wildly into the night, leaving the specter in darkness.

Torrent bent low and whispered to the prisoner, a teenage girl frozen with cold and terror, as he pressed the handle of his knife into her hand and closed her fingers around it. "If he comes in range, don't hesitate. Do you understand?" Soundlessly, she nodded.

He crouched quietly, feeling for his stun baton. He'd dropped it in his hurry to free the girl, and now he couldn't find it. Still he dared not take his eyes off of where he'd last seen the crow-masked man. At last, the wide and limbless outline of that shrouded figure shifted. The gasser lurched forward, hitting that heavy stick against his gloved hand.

"Better run! I'm coming for you!"

"Yeah? Then you better bring more than that stick, shitbird!" Torrent yelled back. Still he groped futilely for the stun baton, knowing that, far away from any source of water, his hydrokinesis wasn't going to help.

His opponent laughed, a deep, barking laughter that Torrent thought oddly theatrical. The gasser strode forward ponderously, his breaths labored and whistling eerily through the beak in his mask. He stopped, planted the pole in the dirt, and drew something from the inside of his cloak. It was a slender wand with a trigger grip on one end. In the dim red light, Torrent barely noticed the thick tube that trailed from it and coiled behind his enemy's back.

Now it was Torrent's turn to laugh. "A squirt gun? What are you going to do, weed me?"

"You're dumber than you look, boy."

Behind Torrent, the captive girl cried out in warning.

"Don't worry, baby. Nothing he's got in there can hurt me," Torrent assured her.

"It's loaded with some kind of chem-" She stopped short as the bird-man raised his weapon, then

immediately rolled over in the dirt, clamping her eyes and mouth shut.

The gasser aimed for Torrent's chest, squeezed the trigger, and then howled in surprise as the wand exploded into a cloud of plastic shrapnel and hissing, foul-smelling vapor. Liquid erupted from the whipping tube, soaking his chest and splashing his face. In a mad panic to keep the noxious fluid off his skin, he tore off the plague mask. His gloved hands slapped at something on his chest and then something heavy and bulky fell off his back and crashed heavily to the ground: the reservoir for his pump-gun, still sloshing with whatever foul-smelling poison he'd bathed the male vagabond with.

Torrent barely managed to dodge the stampeding villain as he darted past, wheezing and retching. Behind Torrent, the captive girl rolled over just in time. Maybe from defensive instinct, maybe from a furious desire to hurt her captor in any way possible, she reached out with one hand and grabbed hold of his ankle.

There was a loud snap, the kind you only ever hear when you step on a dry twig in August. The plague doctor went down shrieking.

Torrent's stomach lurched as he pulled the girl back from the howling maniac. There was a new reek in the air vying with the caustic haze from the squirt gun, something cloying and putrid, the smell of advanced decay, like a carcass swollen up in the summer heat. The stench seemed concentrated around the sickly twisted foot of the plague doctor.

"God, that's awful," Torrent said nasally, holding his breath to fight off the nausea. He looked the girl over. "Nice grab, kid. Keep working on those ankle ties, I have to check on my buddy."

Alex was woozy, but conscious. He had a split lip, a big welt on his cheek, and bloody scratches where the mask buckles bit into his skin, but the filter apparatus of the mask had taken the worst of the blow. The first time he tried to stand up, he immediately toppled sideways so that Torrent had to catch him.

"You better sit down," Torrent said. "I'll zip-tie Miasma while you get your bearings."

"I'm fine. Who?"

"The guy who kicked your ass."

"Bullshit." X spat out some blood. He rolled his head sideways, cracking his neck. "That's his name?"

"That's what I'm calling him. These creeps don't name themselves," Torrent replied.

On his way back to the crippled villain, he spied the handle of his stun baton half-covered in loose gravel. He reholstered it, then made his way over to Miasma. Breathing through his mouth the whole time, Torrent patted him down and zip-tied his hands behind his back. He thought about tying his ankles, too, but Torrent didn't see the point in that, considering how his right foot was bent out at a 90 degree angle. Besides, he didn't want his hands near whatever was making that smell.

Torrent tried to lift him, but found that he couldn't - at least, not without the creep screaming in pain. Beneath the crow mask and the leather cloak, their psycho gasser was hugely corpulent, with overlapping jowls instead of a neck and beady eyes that seemed to be drowning in the flab of his cheeks.

138

Sebastian guessed that he weighed an easy 350. It was no wonder his ankle was totally pulped under that weight.

"What's in the tank, lardass?" Torrent demanded.

Miasma shouted something slanderous about Torrent's mother. The young vigilante fought the temptation to lean on the wounded captive with the shock baton, or better yet, give him a bath in his own chemicals: that was bound to induce a spirit of civility and cooperation. But Torrent's more humane tendencies prevailed.

"Don't move," Torrent warned him.

"I can't feel my leg!" The criminal's voice was fearful and urgent.

"Good. That'll make it easy on you."

Torrent turned round to see the young girl eying him nervously. It was the first time he really got a good look at her. She was skinny - even frail. Her long brown hair was matted and dirty, and she stunk, not with the revolting scent of chemicals, but the natural odors of sweat and damp clothes that had gone too long between washes. Her jeans were ripped up and her tattered brown flannel shirt was covered in old stains. There were still tight loops of rope around her wrists and ankles, but they were no longer tied together.

Torrent smiled easily. "It's OK. You've just been rescued by Torrent and the Mysterious X, Pittsburgh's newest superheroes." He cocked his head toward Miasma. "Don't worry, he's not getting up anytime soon. What's your name?"

Still she didn't say anything, or take her eyes off him. She looked like a rabbit ready to leap, or a cat ready to claw. He belatedly noticed that she still held his knife in her hand.

"Who sent you?" The words were almost hissed through her teeth.

"No one. Are you alright?"

She looked at him sidelong, her voice was tinged with suspicion. "You didn't come looking for me?"

"Uh, not in particular, no."

The vagabond let out a deep sigh of relief. "OK then. I guess you can have your knife back." She stood up and took a step toward him, then paused as if she thought better of it. Instead, she laid the knife on the ground and flashed an exhausted, but genuine smile as she took a step backward.

Torrent narrowed his eyes, wondering at all this. "Hang onto it. It might come in handy."

She raised an eyebrow at him, but didn't hesitate to bend down, fold the knife closed, and slip it into her pocket. "Thanks, chief! I appreciate your help. Really appreciate it. But I have to go." She waved once before turning. "Good luck!"

"Wait! What about your friend-"

"I don't even know him," she called over her shoulder.

"OK, but don't you want to see a doctor?"

"Nope, I'm good. Thanks again!" She took off running down the railroad tracks, and then she was gone.

'This has been a weird week,' he thought.

***

X sat massaging his head when Torrent reappeared. "How's the girl?"

140

Torrent wiped the dirt and mud from his hands onto his pant legs. "I guess she's all right. She's gone already."

"You got the easy one." There was no trace of the second victim but some tatters of rope and an abandoned sneaker. "This is a thankless job," he added.

Torrent gave a low whistle. "You bet."

"Any idea what he was spraying?"

"He wouldn't say. Did your guy have any blisters or burns on him?"

"Not that I could notice."

"Well, there's that," Torrent replied.

"If I had to guess," ventured X, "I'd say it was some sort of psychotic. He sure acted like one."

"DMSO and LSD or something," Torrent mused. He wondered if maybe it was just the rotten smell. He'd heard of old women going crazy from mothball fumes. A smile touched his lips. "Maybe he was just afraid of your goofy mask."

"What are we going to do with Miasma?"

That simple question froze Torrent. Of all the things he'd planned for and worried over, that wasn't one of them. "I don't know," he said, sounding surprised. "I've never taken a prisoner before."

"We should take that psycho gassing son of a bitch's wallet," X suggested. "You know, for compensation."

Torrent shook his head. "No wallet, no mobi. No names or addresses, either," said Torrent. "But I'm sure his fat ass didn't waddle all the way out here with that heavy tank on his back."

"Then he's got to have a vehicle around here," X said.

"We can always ask him."

***

"What the fuck do you want to know that for? You run a chop shop in the day time, you delinquent bastards?" Miasma slobbered with rage.

"So we can find out which asylum turned you loose, you cartoon character," Torrent riposted.

"And for purposes of restitution. You owe me a gas mask," X felt the need to add.

Miasma grunted in understanding, and suddenly his face and demeanor changed. "All right, now we understand each other. Now we can resolve this. I'll give you both $500 to cut me loose. You go home and forget about this, and I get myself to a hospital. How's that?"

"Or we can just take it," Torrent said.

Miasma laughed. "Give me a little credit. I wouldn't bargain with something you can just rob from me. I'll authorize a deposit - cryptographic, not bank scrip. Real, solid money. That's five hundred a piece, not total!"

Torrent and X silently looked at one another. Each was seriously considering the offer, but neither wanted to be the first to say so.

Torrent tapped his partner on the shoulder as he turned away. "We'll discuss this. Privately."

When they put enough distance between them for Miasma's growls to fade into the background, X turned to Torrent. "You want to take the money."

"What? No!" he lied.

142

"Good. Me neither," X said stiffly.

"It *is* a lot of money though," Torrent said. "It'd help us enormously. We could even buy working gas masks."

"Sure could," X muttered. "You know, we *could* smash all of his equipment first. It's not like we'd be giving him a free pass to pull this sick shit again."

A sour look crossed Torrent's face, but it was the chagrin of being reminded what that $1000 was purchasing rather than any disapproval at his friend's mercenary inclination, an inclination that, right now at least, he shared. But his conscience and a well cultivated prudence sounded klaxons of warning - "I'm sure he could make more. He'd be back out when his leg healed."

Abruptly, Torrent decided on something. "I want to find out who he is before we cut any deals with him. Let's look for that car."

The search took about ten minutes to turn up a hopper parked in a rocky clearing on the edge of the railway. It was hastily covered in a black tarp and there was a trace of that familiar, stinging chemical odor around it.

"I guess it's his," X said, sniffing the air. "What do you think? I don't know why anyone would park here."

"Let's look," Torrent said. They flung off the metal weights that held the tarp down and pulled it off the chassis to reveal a faded and weathered dual prop channel-wing in pusher configuration, wings turned up for vertical landing.

"An Aladdin Spindrift," X noted. "This thing's almost as old as I am."

143

"Does Aladdin even exist anymore?" Torrent wondered.

"Nope, they went under about six years ago. My mom used to work at the dealership, remember? Well, it's a beater, but I guess you don't dirty up a flashy luxury flitter with your hobo-gassing equipment."

"I daresay," said Torrent. "Now, here's something interesting." He crouched, examining the transponder attached to the underside of the empennage. Aggravatingly, the city of Pittsburgh required all personal aircraft to fly in established air corridors and pay for an expensive permit/transponder. It was the reason that most people who lived in the city had ground cars, even the ones with hoppers, since they generally kept them parked outside the city limits at the heliports and had to drive to get to them. But it was not just the presence of the transponder that Torrent found curious, but the markings on it.

"It's a municipal tag," he said.

X raised his eyebrows. "What is he, a cop?"

They pried open the unlocked side hatch and went inside the cramped cabin. There was an insurance registration certificate from the ABC made out to a Rodney Jerningham of Zelienople, Pennsylvania. On the seat was a stamped metal case containing a wallet with a state constable's badge.

X swore and punched the roof. "He *is* a cop!"

"Maybe that's why nobody seemed interested in investigating," Torrent suggested. "Maybe he called in a favor, or maybe somebody knew and was covering for him."

144

"I'll be damned if I take his money and let him get away, now. He's an even lower class of scumbag than I thought."

Torrent nodded his head in agreement. "Maybe it won't do any good to turn him in, but then again with all that evidence around, it'll be hard to cover up."

"We should take pictures of all this so it can't be covered up," said X.

Torrent slapped his forehead in frustration. "No kidding! Too bad I didn't bring a camera!"

"That's OK," said X, staring at the insurance certificate. "I'm memorizing that name. Shouldn't be hard to look up."

They put in the call to the railroad instead of the Pittsburgh police on the hope that they might actually get some traction on an arrest and investigation, but not before letting Miasma know that they'd come to a decision.

"Good choice, gentlemen," he rasped. "I knew, as men of the mask like me, we'd work it out. No hard feelings, now."

X answered him with a short kick to the ribs. "No hard feelings, tax-feeder."

Torrent dropped the badge on the back of Miasma's head. "You hold onto that money, constable. Maybe you can bribe the Pinkertons when they get here."

Allegheny Grill

There was no class on April 16, Liberation Day, the commemoration of the lifting of the Martian siege of Pittsburgh. Sebastian was ambling around Squirrel Hill, basking in the light of the waxing sun. It was 70 degrees and cloudless, the kind of day that made northeasterners sigh, look up at the blue sky, and say "Finally!"

Sebastian had traded his long-sleeved dress shirts and thick jackets for a pair of canvas shorts and a New York Highlanders tee. He thought eagerly of the longer and warmer days to come, especially enthusiastic about five months of short skirts and plunging necklines. His secret second life as a costumed vigilante was now far from his mind. Already he'd forgotten about the disturbing encounter with Miasma only a few nights previous. It wasn't that he had a short attention span, just that he had another confrontation to worry about. While less physically dangerous than his midnight extracurriculars, it was a challenge he found more daunting and uncertain than bloody street fights.

It was, in fact, this confrontation that he was trying to delay as he lingered at the crosswalk in front of the Carnegie Library, staring blankly at the blinking 'WALK' sign like a confused Chinese peasant who had never seen an alphabet before. He stepped back onto the curb as the signal went red, turned on his heel, and sucked in his cheeks with a deep gulp of air. He studied his distorted reflection in the library's wall mosaic as if he hoped to find some hidden message, some steganographically obscured encouragement in the coruscating swirls of stained glass, that would defeat his stomach-twisting anxiety. He glanced down at his wristwatch as the minute hand moved past the quarter-hour mark and the inner voice that had been so determined throughout the morning began to counsel surrender.

No, not surrender, he corrected himself, just a reasonable delay. Evangeline's shift ended at two o'clock, and it might take him another 20 minutes to walk to the Allegheny Grill from here, leaving him a mere half-hour during what was bound to be the busiest part of lunch to get her attention, strike up a conversation, and work through his carefully prepared angle, all while she would be hurrying to finish her rounds, clean up, split the tips, and whatever else waitresses did at the end of a shift. It would be better to try tomorrow, earlier in the day when the place would be less crowded or – even better! – wait for that perfect moment with no onlookers and no pressure, when things could develop naturally. They'd meet accidentally on the walk home from school, their paths intersecting serendipitously on a quiet, depopulated side street in Shadyside, the wind gently rustling the young blossoms in the branches above their heads, the tranquil cooing of the pigeons the background music to their hushed conversation. He would offer to carry her bag and escort her home, and she would bashfully accept, and as they walked, the distance between them narrowing with each step, their eyes would linger on one another's until, moved too strongly by instinct to be overcome by fear, their lips would meet in a soft kiss.

How can you rush something like that? You just can't.

Of course Sebastian knew that he was deluding himself, especially since, as far as he knew, Eva was still mad at him. She had done an exceptionally good job of avoiding him for the better part of a fortnight. Nonetheless, his inner coward felt very content with this passive approach. He resolved to forget the plan to make peace with his crush, as well as the deliciously greasy sandwich he'd had his mind on all day and just head home where he could rehearse that tender moment to come with his pillow.

And then, abruptly, one of the private buses that the trendy clubs and shops sponsored to shuttle patrons around a circuit of hotspots from the South Side to Squirrel Hill screeched to a stop in front of him, waiting at the red light. He found himself transfixed by an unusually provocative image glowing from the LCD panel on the bus's flank. It was a young woman, her hair a blonde ziggurat of outrageous height and spangled with ribbons of twisted metal, with smoky eyes behind gold-flecked eyelids fixed in a hard, almost contemptuous glare. Her gaze and her glistening, slightly parted lips seemed a demand of wanton carnality made directly of him. And she was completely naked except for a bizarre ribbon of what looked like interlocking pieces of steel that followed the curving contours just above her waistline, crossed above her navel, and slanted across her shoulders by way of her exceptionally round, cream-colored breasts in a path that just barely obscured her nipples, which Sebastian somehow

148

knew to be very pink and very hard beneath that chain of cold, glittering metal.

His head swiveled to track the shuttle as it rolled on down the street, the dirty thoughts that flooded his head delaying for a few seconds the recognition that it was a billboard for Magnetrix's Great Attractor tour. Magnetrix, the pathetically ineffectual metahuman criminal turned pop tart 'musician' who had inadvertently provoked his rift with Evangeline. Surely it was a sign, but was it a bad omen or was it a prodding reminder that romancing a pillow wasn't going to cut it anymore? He quickly decided that it must be the latter. Now he had all the hormonal encouragement he needed to see Evangeline tonight.

Not quite speed walking, he arrived at the Allegheny Grill quicker than he expected to, whereupon a sudden assault of self-conscious embarrassment nearly convinced him to keep on striding right past the door. Only the certainty that he would be up all night beating himself up in regret over the missed opportunity kept him from doing so.

"Do it now or go through this all over again tomorrow," he said quietly to himself as he pulled open the door.

The interior of the sandwich shop opened up before him in the shape of a backwards "L", with a line of booths running the depth of the building and tables and stools laid out to his left, filling the space between the storefront's streaky glass window and the red-stained oak counter. He made a quick reconnaissance of the place, but didn't immediately spy Evangeline. It wasn't as crowded as he expected, and he felt relieved that at least he wouldn't humiliate himself in front of a lot of people. A moment later he thought he heard her voice echoing from the back, but not wanting to look like he was looking for her, he squinted up at the menu board above the counter, feigning thoughtfulness.

"Can I help you, sir?" asked the big, barrel-shaped man behind the counter. This guy was a true Yinzer: his voice was deep and unnecessarily loud, raspy from too much drinking and smoking. He looked a decade older than he probably was, with deep creases on his pudgy face and more hair on his multiple chins than on the top of his head, but somehow still full of strength and vitality. In short, he looked like he could brain a guy with a full keg of Iron City and then down it all by himself.

"Whoa, hold it! A Highlanders fan?" he mockingly declaimed. "Sorry buddy, we don't serve your kind here."

Sebastian rolled his eyes and hooked his thumb toward the framed Pirates and Strikers posters hung on the far wall and riposted, "Ah, losers only. I get it."

"Hah! Listen to this guy... what'll ya have today?"

"Turkey and bacon on waffles," Sebastian answered enthusiastically.

"Anything to drink?"

"I'll have a medium pop," he replied.

"And here I was thinking that you weren't from around here!" the man said, nodding approvingly. "That'll be three bucks for me and six cents for the man in Harrisburg."

Sebastian paid in cash and then slid into a booth to wait for his food. He sat facing the back of the restaurant on the idea that it was Evangeline's voice he heard coming from the kitchen. There didn't seem to be anyone else bringing out orders or cleaning tables, so with some luck she would be the one bringing his food out. He spent the next several minutes curiously studying a flag encased on the wall above his head. It was a flag of the Confederacy, not the more familiar cross-barred pattern of the battle flag, but the national ensign, the "stars and bars," and evidently ancient as its reds were faded and whites yellowed. Modern day Pittsburgh was pretty cosmopolitan, sitting astride a watercourse that carved out a border among four different countries, so it wouldn't have been unusual to see the flags of any of the American states hanging around, and Lord knows there had always been a lot of Copperheads in Pennsylvania, but this particular flag was remarkable for its vintage. He counted 10 stars on the saltern, which marked it from the 1890s, after the separation of Virginia and Kentucky, the flag as it would've been at the time of the Martian War. He wondered if perhaps an ancestor of the owner had served in the allied army that broke the siege of Pittsburgh and had settled here after the war.

The sound of a plate scuffling across the table and the improbably aromatic mélange of bacon grease, maple syrup, and melted cheese stirred Sebastian from his musings. He glanced up excitedly, but instead of Evangeline, he was face to jowl with the fellow who took his order.

"Here you go, Highlander. You need anything else?"

"Ah… nope, thanks," Sebastian answered, then hesitantly added, "Hey, is there a girl that works here, red hair, thinks pop is called 'soda?' "

"Why yes, I believe there is," the man confirmed, his big droopy eyes humorous. "If you're looking for her phone number, a generous gratuity may induce my cooperation."

"I don't think I'll need any help with that," Sebastian scoffed almost on reflex, but his voice betrayed his nerves.

"Oh ho! Well, I'll tell her you're looking for her."

The big man then left Sebastian to his dinner, though all of a sudden his stomach was doing somersaults and he wasn't hungry anymore.

A few minutes later, Evangeline rounded the counter and stepped slowly down the aisle, glancing uncertainly at the faces of customers for someone she recognized.

"Sebastian!" she said, as if she'd come up with something she'd been trying to remember all day. All the tension of the workday seemed to have left her as she smiled broadly, pale pink lips curving around straight white teeth. "Wow, hi! What are you up to? Besides eating, I mean."

Sebastian had been probing the steaming waffle melt with his fork when she called out to him and he was startled by her ebullience. It was close to the opposite of what he'd expected, and he didn't know how to respond.

"I was just walking around the neighborhood and I was hungry," he eventually said, then hastened to add that she had something to do with his choice, too. "I saw your status that you were working today, so I thought I'd say hi."

"Really?" She looked down nervously for an instant and her voice dropped almost too low to hear. "I'm a little surprised. I didn't think we were friends anymore."

"That was rude of me—"

"I was a jerk," she blurted, and went on talking as if she didn't hear him about to apologize. "I overreacted to what you said and made you out to be the bad guy, and that was really unfair of me. I knew it that night, but I was so embarrassed at how I acted, and you left so mad at me, that I couldn't bring myself to talk to you. I should have apologized, but I was afraid you wouldn't—" Evangeline's tight voice trailed off to silence. She bit her lip.

"No. No way," Sebastian whispered. He stood up and reached out for her hand, squeezing it. "I missed you."

"Yeah?" she said, lifting her wet eyes up to his. "I thought you didn't want to talk to me."

Evangeline tilted her head and smiled a little. "I'm a girl. You were supposed to come after me."

Sebastian laughed, held out his arms. "That's why I'm here."

"You sure took your time!" She took a half-step closer and touched him on the shoulder. "But I'm glad you came. I missed you, too."

Evangeline's mere proximity made his head swim; the warmth of her hand on his arm was almost

too much to bear. Before he knew what he was saying, he blurted: "You get off work at two, right?"

"Yes, I'm finishing up now. Why do you ask?" Her voice was full of an affected coyness.

Sebastian shifted uncomfortably, quiet incoherencies emitting from a mouth still moving faster than his staggered brain. Something cracked inside him, and he let out a self-deprecating chuckle at how ridiculous this all was. He threw up his hands and gave in. "Because I wanted to see if you wanted to do something tonight."

Evangeline's long lashes fluttered over her bright green eyes in exaggerated coquettishness. "Do you mean just with you?"

Sebastian sighed in defeat. "You're making this very hard."

Taking pity on him, Evangeline ended the game. "I'd love to, Sebastian. Where are you taking me?"

He flashed an exhausted smile. "Where do you want to go?"

"You know," she said, hugging herself tightly – and, Sebastian couldn't help but notice, in a way that made her round breasts strain against the white cotton blouse she wore – "It doesn't even matter. Finish eating and think of something."

While he had worked out a multitude of come-ons and hundreds of different lines of conversation, Sebastian belatedly realized that he had no solid plans of where to take her. It was almost as if he expected her to blow him off. He was too happy for that to trouble him, however, and he had his appetite back. When Evangeline returned slightly after two o'clock, he had just finished off the last syrup-slathered strip of bacon. He then uncreatively suggested they check out a movie (he had no preference and didn't even remember what was playing), but she demurred, saying that she preferred to spend the time in a place where they could talk and actually see each other. So, after a fifteen minute walk around the neighborhood filled with pleasant conversation, they settled on a table at a small coffee and dessert shop in Squirrel Hill. Evangeline ordered a cherry slush and Sebastian had a strawberry and banana smoothie, both of which he paid for without any objection from his companion. That made it an official date, he decided.

Their conversation wandered broadly, from their birthdays and hobbies to their thoughts on current events and back to trivial and disconnected observations. They talked about their families, tiptoeing around last month's disastrous dinner with her father. Sebastian was still plenty sore about that episode, but he pressed her for more details of her dad's adventures in the Compass Society, why he quit, and whether he'd done anything exciting afterward. She explained, with notably little appreciation in her voice, that her father did short-term, high-pay stints as a consultant for various companies, requiring them to move often even though it seemed to her that most of his work could be done remotely. The relocation to Pittsburgh had been their third move in as many years. In Deseret, where they last lived, her dad worked for the Mormon church which was attempting to verify some theory about ancient American civilizations.

"Did they?" Sebastian asked with real curiosity.

"I don't know," she shrugged, then added sourly, "Showing interest in my dad's work never paid off for me. The main thing I remember is that the people were nice, but nosy."

"I remember you saying so."

"And strict on themselves. It was hard to find soda out there."

"Pop," he corrected her.

"If you insist," Evangeline replied, noisily slurping the slush through her straw. She held the cup in front of her with both hands, looking at him over the rim somewhat reticently, weighing her words. "So do you get in a lot of fights?" she finally asked.

Sebastian almost choked with surprise, something he didn't think people really did. "What do you mean?" he blurted out, his eyebrows knitting together.

She set the slushie down gently. "That night you came over for dinner you said you'd been hit by a brick. Then you had some bruises on your face and a long cut on your cheek; I can still see them a little bit," she explained and leaned forward, minutely touching a couple of the slightly uneven spots under his eyes with her index finger, "here and here." Sebastian reddened at her touch and his eyes briefly looked away, but Evangeline pretended that she hadn't noticed the reaction and withdrew her hand casually. "Every time I see you, there's a new mark. I wanted to ask you about it a couple weeks ago, but I didn't want to say anything in front of your friends. It seemed like they hadn't noticed that you were wearing makeup, so I didn't want to point it out."

"Well thanks," he said with a sort of astonished look about him, marveling that once again she had caught him off guard. Evangeline, smiling back at him with that playful, but completely confident and self-satisfied expression, was clearly not the tentative and retiring ingénue he had thought she was. Despite the long mental rehearsal for this night, he was prepared only for outright rejection or meek acquiescence, not for the clever and pert young woman that sat before him, and his attraction to her was never more palpable and urgent because of it.

"So I guess I didn't do it so well," he said eventually.

"It makes me happy that you don't know how to put on makeup." She inclined her head, her voice more gentle now. "You don't have to tell me if you don't want to."

Sebastian sighed, surprised that he actually considered telling her the whole story. 'That wouldn't be prudent,' he thought, 'you don't know her that well and it would probably scare her off.' He settled on something more cryptic. "You wouldn't believe me if I told you."

"I probably would." Evangeline once again reflected that innocence and naiveté that Sebastian found more familiar, though at that moment he couldn't have guessed at the depth of her meaning.

"It's not always fights. Sometimes I'm just clumsy," he confessed.

A smile played on her lips. "Why wouldn't I believe that?"

Sebastian let out a little self-conscious laugh and lifted his drink. "You're hurting my self-esteem," he said around the straw.

"I didn't mean it quite like that," she said. "If you do exciting things, you're bound to get injured a little. You just seem like the adventurous type. Heroic."

Sebastian lifted an eyebrow. He knew that he had to tell her.

Appendix

Glossary

Block Government – A government established by and for the residents and property owners of a city block. The trend toward decentralizing governments and localizing rule resulted in many instances of power devolving from large states, to regional governments, to cities, to neighborhoods, and ultimately to individual blocks. These are common in modern cities, particularly in North America and Europe, though their powers and responsibilities differ widely. A form of polycentric law, a step or two away from individual anarchism.

Cog – The common term for what we would call a 'computer'. A shortening of the early 20th century term 'cogitator', which properly referred only to thinking machines.

Eerie – A name occasionally given to the broad category of sensations covered by ESP, psychometry, etc… Especially when the feeling is unsettling or foreboding.

Express – Verb referring to the first manifestation of a paranormal ability. E.g. "My telekinesis didn't express until I was 17."

Flitter – Common slang for a personally owned aircraft. See also **Hopper**.

Grid – A large information and communications network. Essentially, the Ascension Epoch version of the Internet.

Hopper – A personal aircraft. Analogous to the term 'car' for an automobile.

MetaFriends – An online social network, friendly to anonymous users, intended for **Talents**.

Metahuman – A human being with paranormal abilities, especially psionics, not possessed by most other humans. Also known as **Talents**, **Irregulars**, etc…

Mobi – A portable, wearable cog. A very common and important tool as well as a fashionable element in modern clothing.

Moreau - A human/animal chimera created through genetic engineering and/or surgical processes. Named after Dr. Moreau, who created the first such creatures in the late 19th century. Their appearance, behavior, and intelligence vary considerably.

Polycentric Governance/Polycentric Law – A legal structure in which providers of legal systems compete or overlap in a given jurisdiction, as opposed to monopolistic statutory law according to which there is a sole provider of law for each jurisdiction. Often what is really meant by anarchy or statelessness, as opposed to chaos or a lack of dispute resolution mechanisms of any sort.

Psicloban – A psychotropic drug used to suppress certain psychic talents, particularly telepathy and ESP.

Sensitive – A Talent who can detect psychic residue. A broad term that encompasses many forms of ESP, including psychometry, telepathy, teleempathy, etc...

Spoon-bender – A Talent with a useless or very low power ability. Mildly derogatory. (Sorry, Uri Geller!)

Subscription Patrol Service – A type of private security or policing agency that serves its customers based on a subscription model. SPS are popular in many advanced societies, replacing coercively funded police departments. *Troubleshooters, Inc.*, founded by the Target, is an example of a SPS.

Talent - The most commonly used term for a **Metahuman**. Also a term for the paranormal abilities themselves. Coined by Charles Fort.

YOrbit – A popular online social network where people organize their friends, acquaintances, co-workers, etc... in 'orbits' of various distances and levels of interaction with themselves.

John Silence

Dr. John Silence (1882-1976) was a physician and pioneer psychical researcher, famous both for his highly readable personal accounts of encounters with paranormal phenomena and for his theory of Psychic Sinks.

Silence was himself an extra-sensory Talent, possessing psychometry and limited telepathy and clairvoyance (remote viewing) ability. He began his researches in the early 20th century, when the field of psychical research was still closely wrapped-up in occultism and mysticism, and while he disdained the nomenclature and patterns of thought and investigation common to the occultists in favor of the empiricism of science, he did take seriously various "unscientific" and "fringe" subjects as vampirism, lycanthropy, and demonic possession.

His most significant contribution to the field of Talent research is undoubtedly the discovery of Psychic Sinks (or what he called "nullifiers" early on), or people who unconsciously disrupt or negate paranormal activity and actively consume the Psychic Potential Field. Silence hypothesized their existence for years before he was able to prove it (a proof only made possible by the ability to detect and measure the Psychic Potential Field) in the early 1960s. Late in his life, he adopted an orphaned infant Sink, Kelsey Plunkett Silence, to whom he bequeathed all of his materials and wealth.

Inspiration

John Silence was originally created by the incomparable horror and weird fiction novelist Algernon Blackwood. He was the star of six short stories, all of which are now in the public domain. One of these stories, "Ancient Sorceries", is included in this appendix.

Troubleshooter Protective Services

Troubleshooter Protective Services Inc. is a private security company that provides patrol, crime deterrence, and emergency assistance to residential and commercial subscribers. As part this service, the company usually also provides insurance against theft, assault, and other damages to person and property due to criminal acts. Besides their policing duties, Troubleshooters are often found providing other services to subscribers and the community at large, such as collecting mail and feeding pets when a subscriber is out of town, checking in on invalids and the elderly, teaching firearms safety and self-defense, and so on. Every Troubleshooter patrol officer is also trained as an Emergency Medical Technician.

The first and foremost duty of every Troubleshooter is as a peacekeeper, and every employee is trained as such. Since the company must vie for customers in a competitive market, and because Troubleshooters are exposed to the same liability as any other private citizen, the company cannot afford to needlessly offend or recklessly inflict damage on persons or property. Consequently, their training emphasizes de-escalation techniques and non-violent mediation. Although each Troubleshooter patrol officer is equipped with a variety of lethal and less-than-lethal weapons, their incidence of violent confrontations is considerably less than most government police forces. This is partly because the Troubleshooters do not execute search warrants or effect arrests except in public spaces, even when they are empowered to do so. Additionally, every Troubleshooter is required to film their interactions with the public at all times, and any breach of their strict standards of conduct is cause for immediate termination. The Troubleshooters also do not enforce *malum prohibitum* such as laws against underage drinking or unlicensed gambling.

The company is headquartered in Altoona, Pennsylvania, with branch offices serving most of Pennsylvania, Kanawha, western Maryland and Virginia, and northern Kentucky. Founder and CEO Niles Reed earned fame as the non-talent superhero known as the Target, while the chief of the Pittsburgh branch, Tom Foster, was one of his Targeteers.

Rates for residential customers in the Pittsburgh area depend on the local crime rate and other factors, but they can be as low as $20/month, including the premium for crime insurance. The Troubleshooters have more than 30,000 residential customers in the area, and another 5,000 commercial subscribers. The Pittsburgh branch also offers armored transport services (such as for banks and the Carnegie Museum).

The Target and the Targeteers

Niles Reed was as staid and uninteresting as a man could be. He was a lab geek who imagined himself working in an air-conditioned facility under fluorescent lights his whole life and quite content with the idea. He was a materials engineer - and a good one, too: in his late twenties, he invented a novel method of synthesizing spider silk for use in a supple, form-fitting body armor that could resist small-caliber firearms and yet still be light enough to be woven into everyday clothing. Called Silksteel, the fabric was a modest commercial success, but he thought he could do better. With his friend Tom Foster, an electrician and tinkerer, Niles went to work on creating a 'smart' body armor capable of resisting larger-caliber bullets and edged weapons while keeping weight and encumbrance to a minimum. The fabric they came up with was a metallic mesh in a matrix of Silksteel. A network of tiny, embedded microsensors could anticipate an impact and then transmit a small amount of electrical current to turn the flexible metal plates rigid, thus spreading the force of the blow across a much wider area. This new body armor allowed maximum freedom of movement while minimizing the damage due to blunt-force trauma. It was a revolutionary idea; perhaps too revolutionary for investors, who didn't believe the armor could function reliably.

So, Niles did the only thing he could do. He wore the armor and paid someone to shoot him in the chest with a 10mm pistol.

Everyone was very impressed with the armor, and Niles not the least. Niles and Tom got their seed money. But the brush with death awoke something else in Niles, something that would no longer be satisfied by working in a lab.

In the guise of a marketing stunt to help promote their new armor design, Niles fashioned a flashy costume around the armor and a heroic identity to go with it. He called himself the Target and dared petty street criminals, KRAKEN death commandos, and major supervillains alike to shoot him, and he always came out alive.

The Target made enough of a name for himself to run with the Sentinel and some of the other top heroes on the scene. He was one of the first recruits tapped for the Promethean's Project Roundtable, a loose information-sharing and mutual assistance network for independent superheroes. Soon, he was joined by 'Daring' Dave Brown, the guy he'd paid to shoot him in the chest, who also happened to be an Olympic marksman and one of the best tactical shooters on the continent. Eventually, even Tom donned the armor. With Niles' flamboyant showmanship and death-defying stunts, Tom's wisecracking, and Dave's mordant humor and devastating one-liners, Target and his Targeteers were certainly among the most charismatic and popular of the new generation of costumed adventurers.

That was 15 years ago. All three heroes are retired from the superhero gig now - or at least mostly retired. Dave still dawns the suit every once in a while, but Niles and Tom spend most of their efforts training and equipping a whole army of Targeteers, the patrolmen of their private security company, Troubleshooter Protective Services.

Thorpe

Rene Bronson Klocke's mother was a Métis farmgirl from Assiniboia, and his father was a German immigrant machinist who worked the boats on the Great Lakes. That combination made certain things inevitable, like his powerful physique and a love of physical activity. But it also meant his family was in constant motion, moving all around the Union of the Great Lakes and finally to Pennsylvania, and he never seemed to have the time to make any permanent friends. To make things worse, his parents talked funny and he had a weird name. To better fit in, he started calling himself Frank, because "Rene is a sissy name, and Bronson's no name at all." He tried his best to blend in with the sole exception of on the playing field, where his size helped him stand out early. Practically born with skates on, he was a fearless forward in ice hockey, and was soon found to be a quick learner in junior wrestling. He was a first year All Star in the Erie Little League. At Lasky Township School, he made a name for himself as a competitive swimmer and a diver; no one could hold their breath as long as Frank. Needing something to occupy his time in the fall, he took up football, and the track and field coach convinced him to try pole vaulting. Whenever and wherever he had the opportunity to play, he took it.

As he got older, he became less exceptional in size and strength, but only because the other boys started to catch up with him. Stretched thin among so many different sports, others began to exceed him in skill. His baseball coach pointed this out to him one day when he'd been so exhausted from a track and field meet that he gave up three home runs in an inning. Frank knew his coach was right, and it bothered him a little, but not enough to get him to stop. He played for the love of the game — all of them. He wasn't always the most graceful or most thoughtful player, but he was always the most exuberant, and the one thing no one ever beat him for was tenacity.

One night, when he was 16, the track and field team's star hurdler went down with a groin pull. Lasky would have had to forfeit the match and give up their hopes of a regional championship if they didn't find a replacement. Frank had been sidelined for most of the season with his own injuries and had done poorly when he did compete, but he offered to step in anyway. Everybody thought it was a forlorn hope, his coach and teammates included, but Frank put it all on the line. He felt miserable for letting his team down all season and vowed that he'd bring them through no matter the cost to his battered body. Then, in a flash of competitive desperation, just before the starting gun went off, something otherworldly came over him.

Frank won the race, and it wasn't even close. He won despite his injuries and despite not being a hurdler. And he went on winning, all the way to states. Three weeks later, he pitched a perfect game and hit the game-winning home run to clinch the conference final for the school, and that summer his team won the Teen League regionals, too. The next fall, his football team won the conference. He went to

172

the state semi-finals in wrestling and broke a state record in the 500m freestyle. He was named All-Commonwealth in five different sports. Frank was a phenomenon. In an article about Frank's full scholarship to the University of Pittsburgh, a local reporter described him as "athletic excellence incarnate."

The reporter was right, but he should have capitalized the "I". Frank was possessed by an egregore of athletic achievement and became its Incarnate. Frank had no idea about any of this; he simply knew that he was one of the greats, and he was having the time of his life.

He had a great first year at Pitt on both the Track and Football teams, but the school forced him to restrict himself to those two sports lest he burn out or injure himself. Inevitably, Frank continued to seek new challenges - skiing, mountain climbing, cycling, mixed martial arts. His coaches didn't like it at all: they warned him how dangerous it all was, but Frank didn't want to stop. He couldn't. And at the same time, other people began to suspect something was up. That he was a talent (which was true, but not in the way that they suspected), or that he was using booster drugs. Nasty rumors started to spread, and lots of people started digging up dirt.

Frank's downfall came in his junior year, when an illegal bookie was busted and Frank was tied back to him. He admitted gambling, but never on his own matches. They accused him of throwing games. They had no proof of that, but his reputation was ruined. Pitt expelled him and the athletic association banned him for life. The offers from the professional leagues were withdrawn. Frank was exiled in disgrace from the world that he loved.

He felt wronged, betrayed; but he took solace in the story of another one of the all-time great athletes who had been unjustly stripped of his achievements and banned from competition, the incomparable Jim Thorpe. Adopting Thorpe's name as an alias, Frank mocked the university and the news media by leaving his mark on the top floors of the school buildings and offices. Soon he staked his claim on high rises and bridges, defeating and eluding the cops and the anti-graffiti patrols, who, despite their boasting, never once laid hands on him. He satisfied his burning craving for challenge in this way for months, until the night he accidentally ran into a couple of teenage vigilantes. Torrent and X never got any closer to capturing him than anyone else, but they did leave the mark of inspiration on him. Ever since, Thorpe has been one of the Steel City's boldest crime fighters.

Miasma

Police: Former constable is latest victim of hobo brutality
by Kyle Harshaw, Pittsburgh Public Monitor

This morning, city and railway police responded to another report of violence on the railroad, this time near Panther Hollow Bridge in Oakland. The victim, identified as Rodney Jerningham, 49, of Zelienople, was a former state constable. Jerningham was reportedly attacked by a gang of costumed transients who severely beat and then doused him in an unidentified chemical. This would be the fifth incident of transient-related violence in recent days, and the third to involve the use of chemicals. Police are asking that anyone with information about the perpetrators contact them immediately...

A New Wrinkle in the Pittsburgh Gasser Mystery
by Paul Pereira, The Magic Casement

Yet another case of chemical assault in Pittsburgh over the weekend, but with a twist: the victim is an ex-cop, and he claims that hobos did it. Unlike the previous two cases where the victims were hobos themselves, this incident has captured the interest of both police and the respectable media. As usual, however, there are still a couple of details they're ignoring.

First, a reliable source tells me that the latest victim is still in the hospital being treated for a severe case of necrotizing fasciitis - flesh-eating bacteria. Is this the work of the strange chemical? The two previous victims suffered chemical burns, but this is a different animal entirely.

Second, it turns out that the latest victim is not just any ex-cop, but a *disgraced* ex-cop. Rodney Jerningham was fired four years ago during the shake-up at the state crime lab, where he worked as a chemist. He was accused of evidence tampering and the theft of thousands of dollars in supplies, but the Attorney General's office eventually decided to drop the charges against him.

So we have an (allegedly) corrupt chemist wandering the Pittsburgh rail lines at midnight, far from his home, who just happens to become the latest victim of the Gasser. I don't think it crosses the line into libel to say that this is one hell of a coincidence. What say you?

Computer Technology (Cogs)

In the modern day, electronic computers are referred to as **cogs**. Cog is short for 'cogitator', originally the name for a specific type of Martian technology that simulated a conscious, willful intelligence. Although the development of such 'thinking machines' was far outpaced by the development of non-thinking computers, it was these devices that captured the popular imagination early on. They featured prominently in speculative fiction novels and starred even in the earliest days of cinema. As a result, it was 'cog' that became the everyday term for electronic devices when they began to proliferate in the 1960s.

Before cogs were a staple in every home, they were utilized by laboratories and industry. The need to improve cooperation between scattered institutions and increase the utilization of expensive resources led businesses and universities to come up with a variety of schemes to connect computer networks across large geographical distances. This was the beginning of what would be called the Information Grid, or simply the Grid. The development of some common protocols to facilitate exchange between the different Grid sub-networks in the early '70s helped popularize consumer cogs, which were promoted initially as a cutting-edge educational tool for children and a tool to allow office professionals to work remotely. A very competitive consumer market arose, and prices rapidly decreased throughout the decade, until cogs were a common household item in much of the civilized world.

Wearable Computers (Mobis)

'Mobi' was originally a trademark but has since become the genericized term for a type of wearable *cog* (the common term for a computer). A mobi is small, mainly consisting of the battery, CPU, internal memory, and interface adapters. Like most modern devices, mobis can utilize the network cloud for additional processing and storage, and some models having no internal memory. Those more concerned about privacy, or who operate in areas with limited network connectivity, choose models with more powerful onboard storage and processing.

Besides its ultraportability, the key feature of the mobi is that there is no built-in display or interface devices. Instead, it can make wired or wireless connections to most modern devices, like televisions, graphene paper, iGlasses, auggles (augmented reality goggles), projectors, mice, keyboards, styluses, HUDs, microphones, gesture detectors, etc... With the appropriate peripherals and the right software, they can be telephones, mailing servers, navigation devices, personal libraries and theaters, digital companions, media centers, and nearly everything else people find amusing and useful.

Mobis are produced by a huge number of manufacturers with a dizzying variety of specs, the most popular running on open-source operating systems and drivers that are readily customizable.

Modern mobis are usually no heavier than a pound. Easy to carry in a pocket, they are also commonly worn on belts, pinned on collars, and wristbands. As people once wore watches, they now wear mobis. These carrying mounts often incorporate some vital peripherals, like cameras, flashlights, and antennas and wireless range boosters. Because they are so ubiquitous, aesthetics figure prominently in mobi designs. Fashion designers and jewelers often produce high-end mobis with price tags reaching into the tens of thousands of dollars. Average price of a standard consumer mobi is about $30, so most people have more than one, and they are affordable to replace and upgrade.

Personal Aircraft

In the Americas, about half of all passenger miles are traveled by aircraft, but these aircraft are not the large passenger airliners you are used to. Instead, many people own small, private aircraft colloquially called flitters, hoppers, or simply flying cars. These are as simple to fly as an automobile is to drive. Up to distances of about 600 miles, hoppers are even safer than mass-passenger aviation and much more efficient. Beyond that range, traditional airliners, passenger zeppelins, and, at intercontinental ranges, hypersonic ballistic liners fill the need for air travel.

Privately owned personal aircraft have been a significant phenomena since the late 1960s, when the increase in the computing power of cogs and their proliferation to consumer devices made easy-to-fly light aircraft a reality. These were generally fixed-wing craft, larger than the hoppers of today, but more cramped in the cockpit, more expensive, and reliant on standard runways for takeoffs and landings. This limitation restricted their use to the fringes of cities and suburbs where small airports could be found, so some form of ground transportation was still necessary to connect pilots to their planes. Nevertheless, these early personal flyers greatly relieved automobile congestion and mitigated the need for the expansion of expensive and maintenance-intensive highway networks. They were also a good deal safer than automobiles, though they were not used in bad weather.

The advances that would lead to 'backyard' flyers would come a few decades later. The first critical advance was in the sensor suite and flight deck that enabled safe, all-weather flying. Then, in 1987, Swift Motors released the *Phaeton*, a fixed-wing light VTOL. For the first time, consumers had access to a personal aircraft that could take off and land in their driveways. Of course, other VTOL craft like helicopters had been around for decades, but they were extremely noisy and their long blades and rotorwash were extremely dangerous in residential neighborhoods. The key design breakthrough in the Phaeton was its tilting channel wing configuration, a feature that has become common today.

Today, the typical hopper uses channel wings with a pusher prop (the pusher configuration improves safety and cockpit visibility, while the usual performance drawbacks of the configuration are obviated by the position of the prop within the wing channel and the craft's VTOL capabilities) or ducted fans to provide lift and propulsion. Newer models are mechanically simple all-electric designs, running on rechargeable batteries or more expensive but higher endurance LENR systems. Older craft and some high-speed models still use gasoline.

The internal expert systems and sensor suites are every bit as reliable as those found in self-driving automobiles. In fact, even when the pilot is actively engaged, most of the work is still done by the expert system.

Flights in hoppers are extremely safe, and they have a lower rate of serious injury than even commercial aviation, thanks largely to the electronic copilot, which can take over instantly in perilous situations (such as sudden windshear or in anticipation of a collision) and will even prevent the pilot from accidentally doing something stupid when it's "turned off." A whole-craft parachute and flotation rig is standard equipment so that a safe landing is possible even in a catastrophic event like engine loss or collision.

Notable Hopper Makes and Models

- Avro *Windjammer* – four-passenger, twin ducted fan
- Swift Motors *Aeolus* – four-passenger channel wing pusher
- Avro *Galaxy* – unusual four-passenger saucer-shaped with a central rotor and boundary layer control around the rim.
- RWA *Aerius* – five-passenger channel wing pusher
- Rotaplane *Kestrel* – four-passenger channel wing pusher
- Swift Motors *Whisper* – compact two-passenger channel wing pusher
- BMW *1200 series* – high performance four-passenger ducted fan
- Avro *Intrigue* – eight-passenger 'flying van', four ducted fans
- Bensen-Sikorski *Freebird* – four passenger channel wing pusher
- Northeast Aeromotive *Provocateur* – six-passenger 'flying van' dual pusher channelwing

- Hillman *Cadet* – four passenger channel wing pusher
- Martier *Wanderer* – two passenger canard rotor
- International Jumpcraft *T10 series* – two passenger 'flying truck' with cargo bed and four ducted fans

Ancient Sorceries

A John Silence Novelette

by
Algernon Blackwood

First Published in 1908

I

There are, it would appear, certain wholly unremarkable persons, with none of the characteristics that invite adventure, who yet once or twice in the course of their smooth lives undergo an experience so strange that the world catches its breath—and looks the other way! And it was cases of this kind, perhaps, more than any other, that fell into the wide-spread net of John Silence, the psychic doctor, and, appealing to his deep humanity, to his patience, and to his great qualities of spiritual sympathy, led often to the revelation of problems of the strangest complexity, and of the profoundest possible human interest.

Matters that seemed almost too curious and fantastic for belief he loved to trace to their hidden sources. To unravel a tangle in the very soul of things—and to release a suffering human soul in the process—was with him a veritable passion. And the knots he untied were, indeed, after passing strange.

The world, of course, asks for some plausible basis to which it can attach credence—something it can, at least, pretend to explain. The adventurous type it can understand: such people carry about with them an adequate explanation of their exciting lives, and their characters obviously drive them into the circumstances which produce the adventures. It expects nothing else from them, and is satisfied. But dull, ordinary folk have no right to out-of-the-way experiences, and the world having been led to expect otherwise, is disappointed with them, not to say shocked. Its complacent judgment has been rudely disturbed.

"Such a thing happened to *that* man!" it cries—"a commonplace person like that! It is too absurd! There must be something wrong!"

Yet there could be no question that something did actually happen to little Arthur Vezin, something of the curious nature he described to Dr. Silence. Outwardly or inwardly, it happened beyond a doubt, and in spite of the jeers of his few friends who heard the tale, and observed wisely that "such a thing might perhaps have come to Iszard, that crack-brained Iszard, or to that odd fish Minski, but it could never have happened to commonplace little Vezin, who was fore-ordained to live and die according to scale."

But, whatever his method of death was, Vezin certainly did not "live according to scale" so far as this particular event in his otherwise uneventful life was concerned; and to hear him recount it, and watch his pale delicate features change, and hear his voice grow softer and more hushed as he proceeded, was to know the conviction that his halting words perhaps failed sometimes to convey. He lived the thing over again each time he told it. His whole personality became muffled in the recital. It subdued him more than ever, so that the tale became a lengthy apology for an experience that he deprecated. He appeared to excuse himself and ask your pardon for having dared to take part in so fantastic an episode. For little Vezin was a timid, gentle, sensitive soul, rarely able to assert himself, tender to man and beast, and almost constitutionally unable to say No, or to claim many things that should rightly have been his. His whole scheme of life seemed utterly remote from anything more exciting than missing a train or losing an umbrella on an omnibus. And when this curious event came upon him he was already more years beyond forty than his friends suspected or he cared to admit.

John Silence, who heard him speak of his experience more than once, said that he sometimes left out certain details and put in others; yet they were all obviously true. The whole scene was unforgettably cinematographed on to his mind. None of the details were imagined or invented. And when he told the story with them all complete, the effect was undeniable. His appealing brown eyes shone, and much of the charming personality, usually so carefully repressed, came forward and revealed itself. His modesty was always there, of course, but in the telling he forgot the present and allowed himself to appear almost vividly as he lived again in the past of his adventure.

He was on the way home when it happened, crossing northern France from some mountain trip or other where he buried himself solitary-wise every summer. He had nothing but an unregistered bag in the rack, and the train was jammed to suffocation, most of the passengers being unredeemed holiday English. He disliked them, not because they were his fellow-countrymen, but because they were noisy and obtrusive, obliterating with their big limbs and tweed clothing all the quieter tints of the day that brought him satisfaction and enabled him to melt into insignificance and forget that he was anybody. These English clashed about him like a brass band, making him feel vaguely that he ought to be more self-assertive and obstreperous, and that he did not claim insistently enough all kinds of things that he didn't want and that were really valueless, such as corner seats, windows up or down, and so forth.

So that he felt uncomfortable in the train, and wished the journey were over and he was back again living with his unmarried sister in Surbiton.

And when the train stopped for ten panting minutes at the little station in northern France, and he got out to stretch his legs on the platform, and saw to his dismay a further batch of the British Isles debouching from another train, it suddenly seemed impossible to him to continue the journey. Even *his* flabby soul revolted, and the idea of staying a night in the little town and going on next day by a slower, emptier train, flashed into his mind. The guard was already shouting "*en voiture*" and the corridor of his compartment was already packed when the thought came to him. And, for once, he acted with decision and rushed to snatch his bag.

Finding the corridor and steps impassable, he tapped at the window (for he had a corner seat) and begged the Frenchman who sat opposite to hand his luggage out to him, explaining in his wretched French that he intended to break the journey there. And this elderly Frenchman, he declared, gave him a look, half of warning, half of reproach, that to his dying day he could never forget; handed the bag through the window of the moving train; and at the same time poured into his ears a long sentence, spoken rapidly and low, of which he was able to comprehend only

190

the last few words: "*à cause du sommeil et à cause des chats.*"

In reply to Dr. Silence, whose singular psychic acuteness at once seized upon this Frenchman as a vital point in the adventure, Vezin admitted that the man had impressed him favourably from the beginning, though without being able to explain why. They had sat facing one another during the four hours of the journey, and though no conversation had passed between them—Vezin was timid about his stuttering French—he confessed that his eyes were being continually drawn to his face, almost, he felt, to rudeness, and that each, by a dozen nameless little politenesses and attentions, had evinced the desire to be kind. The men liked each other and their personalities did not clash, or would not have clashed had they chanced to come to terms of acquaintance. The Frenchman, indeed, seemed to have exercised a silent protective influence over the insignificant little Englishman, and without words or gestures betrayed that he wished him well and would gladly have been of service to him.

"And this sentence that he hurled at you after the bag?" asked John Silence, smiling that peculiarly sympathetic smile that always melted the prejudices of his patient, "were you unable to follow it exactly?"

"It was so quick and low and vehement," explained Vezin, in his small voice, "that I missed practically the whole of it. I only caught the few words at the very end, because he spoke them so clearly, and his face was bent down out of the carriage window so near to mine."

191

"'*À cause du sommeil et à cause des chats'?*" repeated Dr. Silence, as though half speaking to himself.

"That's it exactly," said Vezin; "which, I take it, means something like 'because of sleep and because of the cats,' doesn't it?"

"Certainly, that's how I should translate it," the doctor observed shortly, evidently not wishing to interrupt more than necessary.

"And the rest of the sentence—all the first part I couldn't understand, I mean—was a warning not to do something—not to stop in the town, or at some particular place in the town, perhaps. That was the impression it made on me."

Then, of course, the train rushed off, and left Vezin standing on the platform alone and rather forlorn.

The little town climbed in straggling fashion up a sharp hill rising out of the plain at the back of the station, and was crowned by the twin towers of the ruined cathedral peeping over the summit. From the station itself it looked uninteresting and modern, but the fact was that the mediaeval position lay out of sight just beyond the crest. And once he reached the top and entered the old streets, he stepped clean out of modern life into a bygone century. The noise and bustle of the crowded train seemed days away. The spirit of this silent hill-town, remote from tourists and motor-cars, dreaming its own quiet life under the autumn sun, rose up and cast its spell upon him. Long before he recognised this spell he acted under it. He walked softly, almost on tiptoe, down the winding narrow streets where the gables all but met over his

192

head, and he entered the doorway of the solitary inn with a deprecating and modest demeanour that was in itself an apology for intruding upon the place and disturbing its dream.

At first, however, Vezin said, he noticed very little of all this. The attempt at analysis came much later. What struck him then was only the delightful contrast of the silence and peace after the dust and noisy rattle of the train. He felt soothed and stroked like a cat.

"Like a cat, you said?" interrupted John Silence, quickly catching him up.

"Yes. At the very start I felt that." He laughed apologetically. "I felt as though the warmth and the stillness and the comfort made me purr. It seemed to be the general mood of the whole place—then."

The inn, a rambling ancient house, the atmosphere of the old coaching days still about it, apparently did not welcome him too warmly. He felt he was only tolerated, he said. But it was cheap and comfortable, and the delicious cup of afternoon tea he ordered at once made him feel really very pleased with himself for leaving the train in this bold, original way. For to him it had seemed bold and original. He felt something of a dog. His room, too, soothed him with its dark panelling and low irregular ceiling, and the long sloping passage that led to it seemed the natural pathway to a real Chamber of Sleep—a little dim cubby hole out of the world where noise could not enter. It looked upon the courtyard at the back. It was all very charming, and made him think of himself as dressed in very soft velvet somehow, and the floors seemed padded, the walls provided with cushions.

The sounds of the streets could not penetrate there. It was an atmosphere of absolute rest that surrounded him.

On engaging the two-franc room he had interviewed the only person who seemed to be about that sleepy afternoon, an elderly waiter with Dundreary whiskers and a drowsy courtesy, who had ambled lazily towards him across the stone yard; but on coming downstairs again for a little promenade in the town before dinner he encountered the proprietress herself. She was a large woman whose hands, feet, and features seemed to swim towards him out of a sea of person. They emerged, so to speak. But she had great dark, vivacious eyes that counteracted the bulk of her body, and betrayed the fact that in reality she was both vigorous and alert. When he first caught sight of her she was knitting in a low chair against the sunlight of the wall, and something at once made him see her as a great tabby cat, dozing, yet awake, heavily sleepy, and yet at the same time prepared for instantaneous action. A great mouser on the watch occurred to him.

She took him in with a single comprehensive glance that was polite without being cordial. Her neck, he noticed, was extraordinarily supple in spite of its proportions, for it turned so easily to follow him, and the head it carried bowed so very flexibly.

"But when she looked at me, you know," said Vezin, with that little apologetic smile in his brown eyes, and that faintly deprecating gesture of the shoulders that was characteristic of him, "the odd notion came to me that really she had intended to make quite a different movement, and that with a single bound she could have leaped at me across the width of that stone yard and pounced upon me like some huge cat upon a mouse."

He laughed a little soft laugh, and Dr. Silence made a note in his book without interrupting, while Vezin proceeded in a tone as though he feared he had already told too much and more than we could believe.

"Very soft, yet very active she was, for all her size and mass, and I felt she knew what I was doing even after I had passed and was behind her back. She spoke to me, and her voice was smooth and running. She asked if I had my luggage, and was comfortable in my room, and then added that dinner was at seven o'clock, and that they were very early people in this little country town. Clearly, she intended to convey that late hours were not encouraged."

Evidently, she contrived by voice and manner to give him the impression that here he would be "managed," that everything would be arranged and planned for him, and that he had nothing to do but fall into the groove and obey. No decided action or sharp personal effort would be looked for from him. It was the very reverse of the train. He walked quietly out into the street feeling soothed and peaceful. He realised that he was in a *milieu* that suited him and stroked him the right way. It was so much easier to be obedient. He began to purr again, and to feel that all the town purred with him.

About the streets of that little town he meandered gently, falling deeper and deeper into the spirit of repose that characterised it. With no special aim he wandered up and down, and to and fro. The

September sunshine fell slantingly over the roofs. Down winding alleyways, fringed with tumbling gables and open casements, he caught fairylike glimpses of the great plain below, and of the meadows and yellow copses lying like a dream-map in the haze. The spell of the past held very potently here, he felt.

The streets were full of picturesquely garbed men and women, all busy enough, going their respective ways; but no one took any notice of him or turned to stare at his obviously English appearance. He was even able to forget that with his tourist appearance he was a false note in a charming picture, and he melted more and more into the scene, feeling delightfully insignificant and unimportant and unselfconscious. It was like becoming part of a softly coloured dream which he did not even realise to be a dream.

On the eastern side the hill fell away more sharply, and the plain below ran off rather suddenly into a sea of gathering shadows in which the little patches of woodland looked like islands and the stubble fields like deep water. Here he strolled along the old ramparts of ancient fortifications that once had been formidable, but now were only vision-like with their charming mingling of broken grey walls and wayward vine and ivy. From the broad coping on which he sat for a moment, level with the rounded tops of clipped plane trees, he saw the esplanade far below lying in shadow. Here and there a yellow sunbeam crept in and lay upon the fallen yellow leaves, and from the height he looked down and saw that the townsfolk were walking to and fro in the cool of the evening. He could just hear the sound of their slow footfalls, and the murmur of their voices floated up to him through the gaps between the trees. The figures looked like shadows as he caught glimpses of their quiet movements far below.

He sat there for some time pondering, bathed in the waves of murmurs and half-lost echoes that rose to his ears, muffled by the leaves of the plane trees. The whole town, and the little hill out of which it grew as naturally as an ancient wood, seemed to him like a being lying there half asleep on the plain and crooning to itself as it dozed.

And, presently, as he sat lazily melting into its dream, a sound of horns and strings and wood instruments rose to his ears, and the town band began to play at the far end of the crowded terrace below to the accompaniment of a very soft, deep-throated drum. Vezin was very sensitive to music, knew about it intelligently, and had even ventured, unknown to his friends, upon the composition of quiet melodies with low-running chords which he played to himself with the soft pedal when no one was about. And this music floating up through the trees from an invisible and doubtless very picturesque band of the townspeople wholly charmed him. He recognised nothing that they played, and it sounded as though they were simply improvising without a conductor. No definitely marked time ran through the pieces, which ended and began oddly after the fashion of wind through an Aeolian harp. It was part of the place and scene, just as the dying sunlight and faintly breathing wind were part of the scene and hour, and the mellow notes of old-fashioned plaintive horns, pierced here and there by the sharper strings, all half

197

smothered by the continuous booming of the deep drum, touched his soul with a curiously potent spell that was almost too engrossing to be quite pleasant.

There was a certain queer sense of bewitchment in it all. The music seemed to him oddly unartificial. It made him think of trees swept by the wind, of night breezes singing among wires and chimney-stacks, or in the rigging of invisible ships; or—and the simile leaped up in his thoughts with a sudden sharpness of suggestion—a chorus of animals, of wild creatures, somewhere in desolate places of the world, crying and singing as animals will, to the moon. He could fancy he heard the wailing, half-human cries of cats upon the tiles at night, rising and falling with weird intervals of sound, and this music, muffled by distance and the trees, made him think of a queer company of these creatures on some roof far away in the sky, uttering their solemn music to one another and the moon in chorus.

It was, he felt at the time, a singular image to occur to him, yet it expressed his sensation pictorially better than anything else. The instruments played such impossibly odd intervals, and the crescendos and diminuendos were so very suggestive of cat-land on the tiles at night, rising swiftly, dropping without warning to deep notes again, and all in such strange confusion of discords and accords. But, at the same time a plaintive sweetness resulted on the whole, and the discords of these half-broken instruments were so singular that they did not distress his musical soul like fiddles out of tune.

He listened a long time, wholly surrendering himself as his character was, and then strolled homewards in the dusk as the air grew chilly.

"There was nothing to alarm?" put in Dr. Silence briefly.

"Absolutely nothing," said Vezin; "but you know it was all so fantastical and charming that my imagination was profoundly impressed. Perhaps, too," he continued, gently explanatory, "it was this stirring of my imagination that caused other impressions; for, as I walked back, the spell of the place began to steal over me in a dozen ways, though all intelligible ways. But there were other things I could not account for in the least, even then."

"Incidents, you mean?"

"Hardly incidents, I think. A lot of vivid sensations crowded themselves upon my mind and I could trace them to no causes. It was just after sunset and the tumbled old buildings traced magical outlines against an opalescent sky of gold and red. The dusk was running down the twisted streets. All round the hill the plain pressed in like a dim sea, its level rising with the darkness. The spell of this kind of scene, you know, can be very moving, and it was so that night. Yet I felt that what came to me had nothing directly to do with the mystery and wonder of the scene."

"Not merely the subtle transformations of the spirit that come with beauty," put in the doctor, noticing his hesitation.

"Exactly," Vezin went on, duly encouraged and no longer so fearful of our smiles at his expense. "The impressions came from somewhere else. For instance, down the busy main street where men and women were bustling home from work, shopping at stalls and barrows, idly gossiping in groups, and all the rest of it, I saw that I aroused no interest and that no one turned to stare at me as a foreigner and stranger. I was utterly ignored, and my presence among them excited no special interest or attention.

"And then, quite suddenly, it dawned upon me with conviction that all the time this indifference and inattention were merely feigned. Everybody as a matter of fact was watching me closely. Every movement I made was known and observed. Ignoring me was all a pretence—an elaborate pretence."

He paused a moment and looked at us to see if we were smiling, and then continued, reassured—

"It is useless to ask me how I noticed this, because I simply cannot explain it. But the discovery gave me something of a shock. Before I got back to the inn, however, another curious thing rose up strongly in my mind and forced my recognition of it as true. And this, too, I may as well say at once, was equally inexplicable to me. I mean I can only give you the fact, as fact it was to me."

The little man left his chair and stood on the mat before the fire. His diffidence lessened from now onwards, as he lost himself again in the magic of the old adventure. His eyes shone a little already as he talked.

"Well," he went on, his soft voice rising somewhat with his excitement, "I was in a shop when it came to me first—though the idea must have been at work for a long time subconsciously to appear in so complete a form all at once. I was buying socks, I think," he laughed, "and struggling with my dreadful

French, when it struck me that the woman in the shop did not care two pins whether I bought anything or not. She was indifferent whether she made a sale or did not make a sale. She was only pretending to sell.

"This sounds a very small and fanciful incident to build upon what follows. But really it was not small. I mean it was the spark that lit the line of powder and ran along to the big blaze in my mind.

"For the whole town, I suddenly realised, was something other than I so far saw it. The real activities and interests of the people were elsewhere and otherwise than appeared. Their true lives lay somewhere out of sight behind the scenes. Their busy-ness was but the outward semblance that masked their actual purposes. They bought and sold, and ate and drank, and walked about the streets, yet all the while the main stream of their existence lay somewhere beyond my ken, underground, in secret places. In the shops and at the stalls they did not care whether I purchased their articles or not; at the inn, they were indifferent to my staying or going; their life lay remote from my own, springing from hidden, mysterious sources, coursing out of sight, unknown. It was all a great elaborate pretence, assumed possibly for my benefit, or possibly for purposes of their own. But the main current of their energies ran elsewhere. I almost felt as an unwelcome foreign substance might be expected to feel when it has found its way into the human system and the whole body organises itself to eject it or to absorb it. The town was doing this very thing to me.

"This bizarre notion presented itself forcibly to my mind as I walked home to the inn, and I began busily to wonder wherein the true life of this town could lie and what were the actual interests and activities of its hidden life.

"And, now that my eyes were partly opened, I noticed other things too that puzzled me, first of which, I think, was the extraordinary silence of the whole place. Positively, the town was muffled. Although the streets were paved with cobbles the people moved about silently, softly, with padded feet, like cats. Nothing made noise. All was hushed, subdued, muted. The very voices were quiet, low-pitched like purring. Nothing clamorous, vehement or emphatic seemed able to live in the drowsy atmosphere of soft dreaming that soothed this little hill-town into its sleep. It was like the woman at the inn—an outward repose screening intense inner activity and purpose.

"Yet there was no sign of lethargy or sluggishness anywhere about it. The people were active and alert. Only a magical and uncanny softness lay over them all like a spell."

Vezin passed his hand across his eyes for a moment as though the memory had become very vivid. His voice had run off into a whisper so that we heard the last part with difficulty. He was telling a true thing obviously, yet something that he both liked and hated telling.

"I went back to the inn," he continued presently in a louder voice, "and dined. I felt a new strange world about me. My old world of reality receded. Here, whether I liked it or no, was something new and incomprehensible. I regretted having left the train so impulsively. An adventure was upon me, and I loathed adventures as foreign to my nature. Moreover, this was the beginning apparently of an adventure somewhere deep within me, in a region I could not check or measure, and a feeling of alarm mingled itself with my wonder—alarm for the stability of what I had for forty years recognised as my 'personality.'

"I went upstairs to bed, my mind teeming with thoughts that were unusual to me, and of rather a haunting description. By way of relief I kept thinking of that nice, prosaic noisy train and all those wholesome, blustering passengers. I almost wished I were with them again. But my dreams took me elsewhere. I dreamed of cats, and soft-moving creatures, and the silence of life in a dim muffled world beyond the senses."

II

Vezin stayed on from day to day, indefinitely, much longer than he had intended. He felt in a kind of dazed, somnolent condition. He did nothing in particular, but the place fascinated him and he could not decide to leave. Decisions were always very difficult for him and he sometimes wondered how he had ever brought himself to the point of leaving the train. It seemed as though some one else must have arranged it for him, and once or twice his thoughts ran to the swarthy Frenchman who had sat opposite. If only he could have understood that long sentence ending so strangely with "*à cause du sommeil et à cause des chats.*" He wondered what it all meant.

Meanwhile the hushed softness of the town held him prisoner and he sought in his muddling, gentle way to find out where the mystery lay, and what it was all about. But his limited French and his constitutional hatred of active investigation made it hard for him to buttonhole anybody and ask questions. He was content to observe, and watch, and remain negative.

The weather held on calm and hazy, and this just suited him. He wandered about the town till he knew every street and alley. The people suffered him to come and go without let or hindrance, though it became clearer to him every day that he was never free himself from observation. The town watched him as a cat watches a mouse. And he got no nearer to finding out what they were all so busy with or where the main stream of their activities lay. This remained hidden. The people were as soft and mysterious as cats.

But that he was continually under observation became more evident from day to day.

For instance, when he strolled to the end of the town and entered a little green public garden beneath the ramparts and seated himself upon one of the empty benches in the sun, he was quite alone—at first. Not another seat was occupied; the little park was empty, the paths deserted. Yet, within ten minutes of his coming, there must have been fully twenty persons scattered about him, some strolling aimlessly along the gravel walks, staring at the flowers, and others seated on the wooden benches enjoying the sun like himself. None of them appeared to take any notice of him; yet he understood quite well they had all come there to watch. They kept him under close observation. In the street they had seemed busy enough, hurrying upon various errands; yet these were suddenly all forgotten and they had nothing to do but loll and laze in the sun, their duties unremembered. Five minutes after he left, the garden was again deserted, the seats vacant. But in the crowded street it was the same thing again; he was never alone. He was ever in their thoughts.

By degrees, too, he began to see how it was he was so cleverly watched, yet without the appearance of it. The people did nothing *directly*. They behaved *obliquely*. He laughed in his mind as the thought thus clothed itself in words, but the phrase exactly described it. They looked at him from angles which naturally should have led their sight in another direction altogether. Their movements were oblique, too, so far as these concerned himself. The straight, direct thing was not their way evidently. They did nothing obviously. If he entered a shop to buy, the woman walked instantly away and busied herself with something at the farther end of the counter, though answering at once when he spoke, showing that she knew he was there and that this was only her way of attending to him. It was the fashion of the cat she followed. Even in the dining-room of the inn, the be-whiskered and courteous waiter, lithe and silent in all his movements, never seemed able to come straight to his table for an order or a dish. He came by zigzags, indirectly, vaguely, so that he appeared to be going to another table altogether, and only turned suddenly at the last moment, and was there beside him.

Vezin smiled curiously to himself as he described how he began to realize these things. Other tourists there were none in the hostel, but he recalled the figures of one or two old men, inhabitants, who took their *déjeuner* and dinner there, and remembered how fantastically they entered the room in similar fashion. First, they paused in the doorway, peering about the room, and then, after a temporary inspection, they came in, as it were, sideways, keeping close to the walls so that he wondered which table they were making for, and at the last minute making almost a little quick run to their particular seats. And again he thought of the ways and methods of cats.

Other small incidents, too, impressed him as all part of this queer, soft town with its muffled, indirect life, for the way some of the people appeared and disappeared with extraordinary swiftness puzzled him exceedingly. It may have been all perfectly natural, he knew, yet he could not make it out how the alleys swallowed them up and shot them forth in a second of time when there were no visible doorways or openings near enough to explain the phenomenon. Once he followed two elderly women who, he felt, had been particularly examining him from across the street—quite near the inn this was—and saw them turn the corner a few feet only in front of him. Yet when he sharply followed on their heels he saw nothing but an utterly deserted alley stretching in front of him with no sign of a living thing. And the only opening through which they could have escaped was a porch some fifty yards away, which not the swiftest human runner could have reached in time.

And in just such sudden fashion people appeared, when he never expected them. Once when he heard a great noise of fighting going on behind a low wall, and hurried up to see what was going on, what should he see but a group of girls and women engaged in vociferous conversation which instantly hushed itself to the normal whispering note of the town when his head appeared over the wall. And even then none of them turned to look at him directly, but slunk off with the most unaccountable rapidity into doors and sheds across the yard. And their voices, he thought, had sounded so like, so strangely like, the angry snarling of fighting animals, almost of cats.

The whole spirit of the town, however, continued to evade him as something elusive, protean, screened from the outer world, and at the same time intensely, genuinely vital; and, since he now formed part of its life, this concealment puzzled and irritated him; more—it began rather to frighten him.

Out of the mists that slowly gathered about his ordinary surface thoughts, there rose again the idea that the inhabitants were waiting for him to declare himself, to take an attitude, to do this, or to do that; and that when he had done so they in their turn would at length make some direct response, accepting or rejecting him. Yet the vital matter concerning which his decision was awaited came no nearer to him.

Once or twice he purposely followed little processions or groups of the citizens in order to find out, if possible, on what purpose they were bent; but they always discovered him in time and dwindled away, each individual going his or her own way. It was always the same: he never could learn what their main interest was. The cathedral was ever empty, the old church of St. Martin, at the other end of the town, deserted. They shopped because they had to, and not because they wished to. The booths stood neglected, the stalls unvisited, the little *cafés* desolate. Yet the streets were always full, the townsfolk ever on the bustle.

"Can it be," he thought to himself, yet with a deprecating laugh that he should have dared to think anything so odd, "can it be that these people are people of the twilight, that they live only at night their real life, and come out honestly only with the dusk? That during the day they make a sham though brave pretence, and after the sun is down their true life begins? Have they the souls of night-things, and is the whole blessed town in the hands of the cats?"

The fancy somehow electrified him with little shocks of shrinking and dismay. Yet, though he affected to laugh, he knew that he was beginning to feel more than uneasy, and that strange forces were tugging with a thousand invisible cords at the very centre of his being. Something utterly remote from his ordinary life, something that had not waked for years, began faintly to stir in his soul, sending feelers abroad into his brain and heart, shaping queer thoughts and penetrating even into certain of his minor actions. Something exceedingly vital to himself, to his soul, hung in the balance.

And, always when he returned to the inn about the hour of sunset, he saw the figures of the townsfolk stealing through the dusk from their shop doors, moving sentry-wise to and fro at the corners of the streets, yet always vanishing silently like shadows at his near approach. And as the inn invariably closed its doors at ten o'clock he had never yet found the opportunity he rather half-heartedly sought to see for himself what account the town could give of itself at night.

"—*à cause du sommeil et à cause des chats*"— the words now rang in his ears more and more often, though still as yet without any definite meaning.

Moreover, something made him sleep like the dead.

III

It was, I think, on the fifth day—though in this detail his story sometimes varied—that he made a definite discovery which increased his alarm and brought him up to a rather sharp climax. Before that he had already noticed that a change was going forward and certain subtle transformations being brought about in his character which modified several of his minor habits. And he had affected to ignore them. Here, however, was something he could no longer ignore; and it startled him.

At the best of times he was never very positive, always negative rather, compliant and acquiescent; yet, when necessity arose he was capable of reasonably vigorous action and could take a strongish decision. The discovery he now made that brought him up with such a sharp turn was that this power had positively dwindled to nothing. He found it impossible to make up his mind. For, on this fifth day, he realised that he had stayed long enough in the town and that for reasons he could only vaguely define to himself it was wiser *and safer* that he should leave.

And he found that he could not leave!

This is difficult to describe in words, and it was more by gesture and the expression of his face that he conveyed to Dr. Silence the state of impotence he had reached. All this spying and watching, he said, had as it were spun a net about his feet so that he was trapped and powerless to escape; he felt like a fly that had blundered into the intricacies of a great web; he was caught, imprisoned, and could not get away. It was a distressing sensation. A numbness had crept over his will till it had become almost incapable of decision. The mere thought of vigorous action— action towards escape—began to terrify him. All the currents of his life had turned inwards upon himself, striving to bring to the surface something that lay buried almost beyond reach, determined to force his recognition of something he had long forgotten— forgotten years upon years, centuries almost ago. It seemed as though a window deep within his being would presently open and reveal an entirely new world, yet somehow a world that was not unfamiliar. Beyond that, again, he fancied a great curtain hung; and when that too rolled up he would see still farther into this region and at last understand something of the secret life of these extraordinary people.

"Is this why they wait and watch?" he asked himself with rather a shaking heart, "for the time when I shall join them—or refuse to join them? Does the decision rest with me after all, and not with them?"

And it was at this point that the sinister character of the adventure first really declared itself, and he became genuinely alarmed. The stability of his rather fluid little personality was at stake, he felt, and something in his heart turned coward.

Why otherwise should he have suddenly taken to walking stealthily, silently, making as little sound as possible, for ever looking behind him? Why else should he have moved almost on tiptoe about the passages of the practically deserted inn, and when he was abroad have found himself deliberately taking advantage of what cover presented itself? And why, if he was not afraid, should the wisdom of staying indoors after sundown have suddenly occurred to him as eminently desirable? Why, indeed?

And, when John Silence gently pressed him for an explanation of these things, he admitted apologetically that he had none to give.

"It was simply that I feared something might happen to me unless I kept a sharp look-out. I felt afraid. It was instinctive," was all he could say. "I got the impression that the whole town was after me—wanted me for something; and that if it got me I should lose myself, or at least the Self I knew, in some unfamiliar state of consciousness. But I am not a psychologist, you know," he added meekly, "and I cannot define it better than that."

It was while lounging in the courtyard half an hour before the evening meal that Vezin made this discovery, and he at once went upstairs to his quiet room at the end of the winding passage to think it over alone. In the yard it was empty enough, true, but there was always the possibility that the big woman whom he dreaded would come out of some door, with her pretence of knitting, to sit and watch him. This had happened several times, and he could not endure the sight of her. He still remembered his original fancy, bizarre though it was, that she would spring upon him the moment his back was turned and land with one single crushing leap upon his neck. Of course it was nonsense, but then it haunted him, and once an idea begins to do that it ceases to be nonsense. It has clothed itself in reality.

He went upstairs accordingly. It was dusk, and the oil lamps had not yet been lit in the passages. He stumbled over the uneven surface of the ancient flooring, passing the dim outlines of doors along the corridor—doors that he had never once seen opened—rooms that seemed never occupied. He moved, as his habit now was, stealthily and on tiptoe.

Half-way down the last passage to his own chamber there was a sharp turn, and it was just here, while groping round the walls with outstretched hands, that his fingers touched something that was not wall—something that moved. It was soft and warm in texture, indescribably fragrant, and about the height of his shoulder; and he immediately thought of a furry, sweet-smelling kitten. The next minute he knew it was something quite different.

Instead of investigating, however,—his nerves must have been too overwrought for that, he said,—he shrank back as closely as possible against the wall on the other side. The thing, whatever it was, slipped past him with a sound of rustling and, retreating with light footsteps down the passage behind him, was gone. A breath of warm, scented air was wafted to his nostrils.

Vezin caught his breath for an instant and paused, stockstill, half leaning against the wall—and then almost ran down the remaining distance and entered his room with a rush, locking the door hurriedly behind him. Yet it was not fear that made him run: it was excitement, pleasurable excitement. His nerves were tingling, and a delicious glow made itself felt all over his body. In a flash it came to him that this was

212

just what he had felt twenty-five years ago as a boy when he was in love for the first time. Warm currents of life ran all over him and mounted to his brain in a whirl of soft delight. His mood was suddenly become tender, melting, loving.

The room was quite dark, and he collapsed upon the sofa by the window, wondering what had happened to him and what it all meant. But the only thing he understood clearly in that instant was that something in him had swiftly, magically changed: he no longer wished to leave, or to argue with himself about leaving. The encounter in the passage-way had changed all that. The strange perfume of it still hung about him, bemusing his heart and mind. For he knew that it was a girl who had passed him, a girl's face that his fingers had brushed in the darkness, and he felt in some extraordinary way as though he had been actually kissed by her, kissed full upon the lips.

Trembling, he sat upon the sofa by the window and struggled to collect his thoughts. He was utterly unable to understand how the mere passing of a girl in the darkness of a narrow passage-way could communicate so electric a thrill to his whole being that he still shook with the sweetness of it. Yet, there it was! And he found it as useless to deny as to attempt analysis. Some ancient fire had entered his veins, and now ran coursing through his blood; and that he was forty-five instead of twenty did not matter one little jot. Out of all the inner turmoil and confusion emerged the one salient fact that the mere atmosphere, the merest casual touch, of this girl, unseen, unknown in the darkness, had been sufficient to stir dormant fires in the centre of his heart, and rouse his whole being from a state of feeble sluggishness to one of tearing and tumultuous excitement.

After a time, however, the number of Vezin's years began to assert their cumulative power; he grew calmer, and when a knock came at length upon his door and he heard the waiter's voice suggesting that dinner was nearly over, he pulled himself together and slowly made his way downstairs into the dining-room.

Every one looked up as he entered, for he was very late, but he took his customary seat in the far corner and began to eat. The trepidation was still in his nerves, but the fact that he had passed through the courtyard and hall without catching sight of a petticoat served to calm him a little. He ate so fast that he had almost caught up with the current stage of the table d'hôte, when a slight commotion in the room drew his attention.

His chair was so placed that the door and the greater portion of the long *salle à manger* were behind him, yet it was not necessary to turn round to know that the same person he had passed in the dark passage had now come into the room. He felt the presence long before he heard or saw any one. Then he became aware that the old men, the only other guests, were rising one by one in their places, and exchanging greetings with some one who passed among them from table to table. And when at length he turned with his heart beating furiously to ascertain for himself, he saw the form of a young girl, lithe and slim, moving down the centre of the room and making straight for his own table in the corner. She moved wonderfully, with sinuous grace, like a young panther, and her approach filled him with such delicious bewilderment that he was utterly unable to tell at first what her face was like, or discover what it was about the whole presentment of the creature that filled him anew with trepidation and delight.

"Ah, Ma'mselle est de retour!" he heard the old waiter murmur at his side, and he was just able to take in that she was the daughter of the proprietress, when she was upon him, and he heard her voice. She was addressing him. Something of red lips he saw and laughing white teeth, and stray wisps of fine dark hair about the temples; but all the rest was a dream in which his own emotion rose like a thick cloud before his eyes and prevented his seeing accurately, or knowing exactly what he did. He was aware that she greeted him with a charming little bow; that her beautiful large eyes looked searchingly into his own; that the perfume he had noticed in the dark passage again assailed his nostrils, and that she was bending a little towards him and leaning with one hand on the table at this side. She was quite close to him—that was the chief thing he knew—explaining that she had been asking after the comfort of her mother's guests, and now was introducing herself to the latest arrival—himself.

"M'sieur has already been here a few days," he heard the waiter say; and then her own voice, sweet as singing, replied—

"Ah, but M'sieur is not going to leave us just yet, I hope. My mother is too old to look after the comfort of our guests properly, but now I am here I will

215

remedy all that." She laughed deliciously. "M'sieur shall be well looked after."

Vezin, struggling with his emotion and desire to be polite, half rose to acknowledge the pretty speech, and to stammer some sort of reply, but as he did so his hand by chance touched her own that was resting upon the table, and a shock that was for all the world like a shock of electricity, passed from her skin into his body. His soul wavered and shook deep within him. He caught her eyes fixed upon his own with a look of most curious intentness, and the next moment he knew that he had sat down wordless again on his chair, that the girl was already half-way across the room, and that he was trying to eat his salad with a dessert-spoon and a knife.

Longing for her return, and yet dreading it, he gulped down the remainder of his dinner, and then went at once to his bedroom to be alone with his thoughts. This time the passages were lighted, and he suffered no exciting contretemps; yet the winding corridor was dim with shadows, and the last portion, from the bend of the walls onwards, seemed longer than he had ever known it. It ran downhill like the pathway on a mountain side, and as he tiptoed softly down it he felt that by rights it ought to have led him clean out of the house into the heart of a great forest. The world was singing with him. Strange fancies filled his brain, and once in the room, with the door securely locked, he did not light the candles, but sat by the open window thinking long, long thoughts that came unbidden in troops to his mind.

IV

This part of the story he told to Dr. Silence, without special coaxing, it is true, yet with much stammering embarrassment. He could not in the least understand, he said, how the girl had managed to affect him so profoundly, and even before he had set eyes upon her. For her mere proximity in the darkness had been sufficient to set him on fire. He knew nothing of enchantments, and for years had been a stranger to anything approaching tender relations with any member of the opposite sex, for he was encased in shyness, and realised his overwhelming defects only too well. Yet this bewitching young creature came to him deliberately. Her manner was unmistakable, and she sought him out on every possible occasion. Chaste and sweet she was undoubtedly, yet frankly inviting; and she won him utterly with the first glance of her shining eyes, even if she had not already done so in the dark merely by the magic of her invisible presence.

"You felt she was altogether wholesome and good!" queried the doctor. "You had no reaction of any sort—for instance, of alarm?"

Vezin looked up sharply with one of his inimitable little apologetic smiles. It was some time before he replied. The mere memory of the adventure had suffused his shy face with blushes, and his brown eyes sought the floor again before he answered.

"I don't think I can quite say that," he explained presently. "I acknowledged certain qualms, sitting up in my room afterwards. A conviction grew upon me that there was something about her—how shall I express it?—well, something unholy. It is not impurity in any sense, physical or mental, that I mean, but something quite indefinable that gave me a vague sensation of the creeps. She drew me, and at the same time repelled me, more than—than—"

He hesitated, blushing furiously, and unable to finish the sentence.

"Nothing like it has ever come to me before or since," he concluded, with lame confusion. "I suppose it was, as you suggested just now, something of an enchantment. At any rate, it was strong enough to make me feel that I would stay in that awful little haunted town for years if only I could see her every day, hear her voice, watch her wonderful movements, and sometimes, perhaps, touch her hand."

"Can you explain to me what you felt was the source of her power?" John Silence asked, looking purposely anywhere but at the narrator.

"I am surprised that you should ask me such a question," answered Vezin, with the nearest approach to dignity he could manage. "I think no man can describe to another convincingly wherein lies the magic of the woman who ensnares him. I certainly cannot. I can only say this slip of a girl bewitched me, and the mere knowledge that she was living and sleeping in the same house filled me with an extraordinary sense of delight.

"But there's one thing I can tell you," he went on earnestly, his eyes aglow, "namely, that she seemed to sum up and synthesise in herself all the strange hidden forces that operated so mysteriously in the town and its inhabitants. She had the silken movements of the panther, going smoothly, silently to and fro, and the same indirect, oblique methods as the townsfolk, screening, like them, secret purposes of her own—purposes that I was sure had *me* for their objective. She kept me, to my terror and delight, ceaselessly under observation, yet so carelessly, so consummately, that another man less sensitive, if I may say so"—he made a deprecating gesture—"or less prepared by what had gone before, would never have noticed it at all. She was always still, always reposeful, yet she seemed to be everywhere at once, so that I never could escape from her. I was continually meeting the stare and laughter of her great eyes, in the corners of the rooms, in the passages, calmly looking at me through the windows, or in the busiest parts of the public streets."

Their intimacy, it seems, grew very rapidly after this first encounter which had so violently disturbed the little man's equilibrium. He was naturally very prim, and prim folk live mostly in so small a world that anything violently unusual may shake them clean out of it, and they therefore instinctively distrust originality. But Vezin began to forget his primness after awhile. The girl was always modestly behaved, and as her mother's representative she naturally had to do with the guests in the hotel. It was not out of the way that a spirit of camaraderie should spring up. Besides, she was young, she was charmingly pretty, she was French, and—she obviously liked him.

At the same time, there was something indescribable—a certain indefinable atmosphere of other places, other times—that made him try hard to remain on his guard, and sometimes made him catch his breath with a sudden start. It was all rather like a delirious dream, half delight, half dread, he confided in a whisper to Dr. Silence; and more than once he hardly knew quite what he was doing or saying, as though he were driven forward by impulses he scarcely recognised as his own.

And though the thought of leaving presented itself again and again to his mind, it was each time with less insistence, so that he stayed on from day to day, becoming more and more a part of the sleepy life of this dreamy mediaeval town, losing more and more of his recognisable personality. Soon, he felt, the Curtain within would roll up with an awful rush, and he would find himself suddenly admitted into the secret purposes of the hidden life that lay behind it all. Only, by that time, he would have become transformed into an entirely different being.

And, meanwhile, he noticed various little signs of the intention to make his stay attractive to him: flowers in his bedroom, a more comfortable arm-chair in the corner, and even special little extra dishes on his private table in the dining-room. Conversations, too, with "Mademoiselle Ilsé" became more and more frequent and pleasant, and although they seldom travelled beyond the weather, or the details of the town, the girl, he noticed, was never in a hurry to bring them to an end, and often contrived to interject little odd sentences that he never properly understood, yet felt to be significant.

And it was these stray remarks, full of a meaning that evaded him, that pointed to some hidden purpose of her own and made him feel uneasy. They all had to do, he felt sure, with reasons for his staying on in the town indefinitely.

"And has M'sieur not even yet come to a decision?" she said softly in his ear, sitting beside him in the sunny yard before *déjeuner*, the acquaintance having progressed with significant rapidity. "Because, if it's so difficult, we must all try together to help him!"

The question startled him, following upon his own thoughts. It was spoken with a pretty laugh, and a stray bit of hair across one eye, as she turned and peered at him half roguishly. Possibly he did not quite understand the French of it, for her near presence always confused his small knowledge of the language distressingly. Yet the words, and her manner, and something else that lay behind it all in her mind, frightened him. It gave such point to his feeling that the town was waiting for him to make his mind up on some important matter.

At the same time, her voice, and the fact that she was there so close beside him in her soft dark dress, thrilled him inexpressibly.

"It is true I find it difficult to leave," he stammered, losing his way deliciously in the depths of her eyes, "and especially now that Mademoiselle Ilsé has come."

He was surprised at the success of his sentence, and quite delighted with the little gallantry of it. But at the same time he could have bitten his tongue off for having said it.

"Then after all you like our little town, or you would not be pleased to stay on," she said, ignoring the compliment.

"I am enchanted with it, and enchanted with you," he cried, feeling that his tongue was somehow slipping beyond the control of his brain. And he was on the verge of saying all manner of other things of

221

the wildest description, when the girl sprang lightly up from her chair beside him, and made to go.

"It is *soupe à l'onion* to-day!" she cried, laughing back at him through the sunlight, "and I must go and see about it. Otherwise, you know, M'sieur will not enjoy his dinner, and then, perhaps, he will leave us!"

He watched her cross the courtyard, moving with all the grace and lightness of the feline race, and her simple black dress clothed her, he thought, exactly like the fur of the same supple species. She turned once to laugh at him from the porch with the glass door, and then stopped a moment to speak to her mother, who sat knitting as usual in her corner seat just inside the hall-way.

But how was it, then, that the moment his eye fell upon this ungainly woman, the pair of them appeared suddenly as other than they were? Whence came that transforming dignity and sense of power that enveloped them both as by magic? What was it about that massive woman that made her appear instantly regal, and set her on a throne in some dark and dreadful scenery, wielding a sceptre over the red glare of some tempestuous orgy? And why did this slender stripling of a girl, graceful as a willow, lithe as a young leopard, assume suddenly an air of sinister majesty, and move with flame and smoke about her head, and the darkness of night beneath her feet?

Vezin caught his breath and sat there transfixed. Then, almost simultaneously with its appearance, the queer notion vanished again, and the sunlight of day caught them both, and he heard her laughing to her mother about the *soupe à l'onion*, and saw her glancing back at him over her dear little shoulder with a smile that made him think of a dew-kissed rose bending lightly before summer airs.

And, indeed, the onion soup was particularly excellent that day, because he saw another cover laid at his small table, and, with fluttering heart, heard the waiter murmur by way of explanation that "Ma'mselle Ilsé would honour M'sieur to-day at *déjeuner*, as her custom sometimes is with her mother's guests."

So actually she sat by him all through that delirious meal, talking quietly to him in easy French, seeing that he was well looked after, mixing the salad-dressing, and even helping him with her own hand. And, later in the afternoon, while he was smoking in the courtyard, longing for a sight of her as soon as her duties were done, she came again to his side, and when he rose to meet her, she stood facing him a moment, full of a perplexing sweet shyness before she spoke—

"My mother thinks you ought to know more of the beauties of our little town, and *I* think so too! Would M'sieur like me to be his guide, perhaps? I can show him everything, for our family has lived here for many generations."

She had him by the hand, indeed, before he could find a single word to express his pleasure, and led him, all unresisting, out into the street, yet in such a way that it seemed perfectly natural she should do so, and without the faintest suggestion of boldness or immodesty. Her face glowed with the pleasure and interest of it, and with her short dress and tumbled hair she looked every bit the charming child of seventeen that she was, innocent and playful, proud of her native town, and alive beyond her years to the sense of its ancient beauty.

So they went over the town together, and she showed him what she considered its chief interest: the tumble-down old house where her forebears had lived; the sombre, aristocratic-looking mansion where her mother's family dwelt for centuries, and the ancient market-place where several hundred years before the witches had been burnt by the score. She kept up a lively running stream of talk about it all, of which he understood not a fiftieth part as he trudged along by her side, cursing his forty-five years and feeling all the yearnings of his early manhood revive and jeer at him. And, as she talked, England and Surbiton seemed very far away indeed, almost in another age of the world's history. Her voice touched something immeasurably old in him, something that slept deep. It lulled the surface parts of his consciousness to sleep, allowing what was far more ancient to awaken. Like the town, with its elaborate pretence of modern active life, the upper layers of his being became dulled, soothed, muffled, and what lay underneath began to stir in its sleep. That big Curtain swayed a little to and fro. Presently it might lift altogether....

He began to understand a little better at last. The mood of the town was reproducing itself in him. In proportion as his ordinary external self became muffled, that inner secret life, that was far more real and vital, asserted itself. And this girl was surely the high-priestess of it all, the chief instrument of its accomplishment. New thoughts, with new interpretations, flooded his mind as she walked beside him through the winding streets, while the picturesque old gabled town, softly coloured in the sunset, had never appeared to him so wholly wonderful and seductive.

And only one curious incident came to disturb and puzzle him, slight in itself, but utterly inexplicable, bringing white terror into the child's face and a scream to her laughing lips. He had merely pointed to a column of blue smoke that rose from the burning autumn leaves and made a picture against the red roofs, and had then run to the wall and called her to his side to watch the flames shooting here and there through the heap of rubbish. Yet, at the sight of it, as though taken by surprise, her face had altered dreadfully, and she had turned and run like the wind, calling out wild sentences to him as she ran, of which he had not understood a single word, except that the fire apparently frightened her, and she wanted to get quickly away from it, and to get him away too.

Yet five minutes later she was as calm and happy again as though nothing had happened to alarm or waken troubled thoughts in her, and they had both forgotten the incident.

They were leaning over the ruined ramparts together listening to the weird music of the band as he had heard it the first day of his arrival. It moved him again profoundly as it had done before, and somehow he managed to find his tongue and his best French. The girl leaned across the stones close beside him. No one was about. Driven by some remorseless engine within he began to stammer something—he hardly knew what—of his strange admiration for her. Almost at the first word she sprang lightly off the wall and came up smiling in front of him, just touching his knees as he sat there. She was hatless as usual, and the sun caught her hair and one side of her cheek and throat.

"Oh, I'm so glad!" she cried, clapping her little hands softly in his face, "so very glad, because that means that if you like me you must also like what I do, and what I belong to."

Already he regretted bitterly having lost control of himself. Something in the phrasing of her sentence chilled him. He knew the fear of embarking upon an unknown and dangerous sea.

"You will take part in our real life, I mean," she added softly, with an indescribable coaxing of manner, as though she noticed his shrinking. "You will come back to us."

Already this slip of a child seemed to dominate him; he felt her power coming over him more and more; something emanated from her that stole over his senses and made him aware that her personality, for all its simple grace, held forces that were stately, imposing, august. He saw her again moving through smoke and flame amid broken and tempestuous scenery, alarmingly strong, her terrible mother by her side. Dimly this shone through her smile and appearance of charming innocence.

"You will, I know," she repeated, holding him with her eyes.

They were quite alone up there on the ramparts, and the sensation that she was overmastering him stirred a wild sensuousness in his blood. The mingled abandon and reserve in her attracted him furiously, and all of him that was man rose up and resisted the creeping influence, at the same time acclaiming it with the full delight of his forgotten youth. An irresistible desire came to him to question her, to summon what still remained to him of his own little personality in an effort to retain the right to his normal self.

The girl had grown quiet again, and was now leaning on the broad wall close beside him, gazing out across the darkening plain, her elbows on the coping, motionless as a figure carved in stone. He took his courage in both hands.

"Tell me, Ilsé," he said, unconsciously imitating her own purring softness of voice, yet aware that he was utterly in earnest, "what is the meaning of this town, and what is this real life you speak of? And why is it that the people watch me from morning to night? Tell me what it all means? And, tell me," he added more quickly with passion in his voice, "what you really are—yourself?"

She turned her head and looked at him through half-closed eyelids, her growing inner excitement betraying itself by the faint colour that ran like a shadow across her face.

"It seems to me,"—he faltered oddly under her gaze—"that I have some right to know—"

Suddenly she opened her eyes to the full. "You love me, then?" she asked softly.

"I swear," he cried impetuously, moved as by the force of a rising tide, "I never felt before—I have never known any other girl who—"

"Then you *have* the right to know," she calmly interrupted his confused confession, "for love shares all secrets."

She paused, and a thrill like fire ran swiftly through him. Her words lifted him off the earth, and he felt a radiant happiness, followed almost the same instant in horrible contrast by the thought of death. He became aware that she had turned her eyes upon his own and was speaking again.

"The real life I speak of," she whispered, "is the old, old life within, the life of long ago, the life to which you, too, once belonged, and to which you still belong."

A faint wave of memory troubled the deeps of his soul as her low voice sank into him. What she was saying he knew instinctively to be true, even though he could not as yet understand its full purport. His present life seemed slipping from him as he listened, merging his personality in one that was far older and greater. It was this loss of his present self that brought to him the thought of death.

"You came here," she went on, "with the purpose of seeking it, and the people felt your presence and are waiting to know what you decide, whether you will leave them without having found it, or whether—"

Her eyes remained fixed upon his own, but her face began to change, growing larger and darker with an expression of age.

"It is their thoughts constantly playing about your soul that makes you feel they watch you. They do not watch you with their eyes. The purposes of their inner life are calling to you, seeking to claim you. You were all part of the same life long, long ago, and now they want you back again among them."

Vezin's timid heart sank with dread as he listened; but the girl's eyes held him with a net of joy so that he had no wish to escape. She fascinated him, as it were, clean out of his normal self.

"Alone, however, the people could never have caught and held you," she resumed. "The motive force was not strong enough; it has faded through all these years. But I"—she paused a moment and looked at him with complete confidence in her splendid eyes— "I possess the spell to conquer you and hold you: the spell of old love. I can win you back again and make you live the old life with me, for the force of the ancient tie between us, if I choose to use it, is irresistible. And I do choose to use it. I still want you. And you, dear soul of my dim past"—she pressed closer to him so that her breath passed across his eyes, and her voice positively sang—"I mean to have you, for you love me and are utterly at my mercy."

Vezin heard, and yet did not hear; understood, yet did not understand. He had passed into a condition of exaltation. The world was beneath his feet, made of music and flowers, and he was flying somewhere far above it through the sunshine of pure delight. He was breathless and giddy with the wonder of her words. They intoxicated him. And, still, the terror of it all, the dreadful thought of death, pressed ever behind her sentences. For flames shot through her voice out of black smoke and licked at his soul.

And they communicated with one another, it seemed to him, by a process of swift telepathy, for his French could never have compassed all he said to her. Yet she understood perfectly, and what she said to him was like the recital of verses long since known.

229

And the mingled pain and sweetness of it as he listened were almost more than his little soul could hold.

"Yet I came here wholly by chance—" he heard himself saying.

"No," she cried with passion, "you came here because I called to you. I have called to you for years, and you came with the whole force of the past behind you. You had to come, for I own you, and I claim you."

She rose again and moved closer, looking at him with a certain insolence in the face—the insolence of power.

The sun had set behind the towers of the old cathedral and the darkness rose up from the plain and enveloped them. The music of the band had ceased. The leaves of the plane trees hung motionless, but the chill of the autumn evening rose about them and made Vezin shiver. There was no sound but the sound of their voices and the occasional soft rustle of the girl's dress. He could hear the blood rushing in his ears. He scarcely realised where he was or what he was doing. Some terrible magic of the imagination drew him deeply down into the tombs of his own being, telling him in no unfaltering voice that her words shadowed forth the truth. And this simple little French maid, speaking beside him with so strange authority, he saw curiously alter into quite another being. As he stared into her eyes, the picture in his mind grew and lived, dressing itself vividly to his inner vision with a degree of reality he was compelled to acknowledge. As once before, he saw her tall and stately, moving through wild and broken scenery of forests and mountain caverns, the glare of flames behind her head and clouds of shifting smoke about her feet. Dark leaves encircled her hair, flying loosely in the wind, and her limbs shone through the merest rags of clothing. Others were about her, too, and ardent eyes on all sides cast delirious glances upon her, but her own eyes were always for One only, one whom she held by the hand. For she was leading the dance in some tempestuous orgy to the music of chanting voices, and the dance she led circled about a great and awful Figure on a throne, brooding over the scene through lurid vapours, while innumerable other wild faces and forms crowded furiously about her in the dance. But the one she held by the hand he knew to be himself, and the monstrous shape upon the throne he knew to be her mother.

The vision rose within him, rushing to him down the long years of buried time, crying aloud to him with the voice of memory reawakened.... And then the scene faded away and he saw the clear circle of the girl's eyes gazing steadfastly into his own, and she became once more the pretty little daughter of the innkeeper, and he found his voice again.

"And you," he whispered tremblingly—"you child of visions and enchantment, how is it that you so bewitch me that I loved you even before I saw?"

She drew herself up beside him with an air of rare dignity.

"The call of the Past," she said; "and besides," she added proudly, "in the real life I am a princess—"

"A princess!" he cried.

"—and my mother is a queen!"

At this, little Vezin utterly lost his head. Delight tore at his heart and swept him into sheer ecstasy. To hear that sweet singing voice, and to see those adorable little lips utter such things, upset his balance beyond all hope of control. He took her in his arms and covered her unresisting face with kisses.

But even while he did so, and while the hot passion swept him, he felt that she was soft and loathsome, and that her answering kisses stained his very soul.... And when, presently, she had freed herself and vanished into the darkness, he stood there, leaning against the wall in a state of collapse, creeping with horror from the touch of her yielding body, and inwardly raging at the weakness that he already dimly realised must prove his undoing.

And from the shadows of the old buildings into which she disappeared there rose in the stillness of the night a singular, long-drawn cry, which at first he took for laughter, but which later he was sure he recognised as the almost human wailing of a cat.

V

For a long time Vezin leant there against the wall, alone with his surging thoughts and emotions. He understood at length that he had done the one thing necessary to call down upon him the whole force of this ancient Past. For in those passionate kisses he had acknowledged the tie of olden days, and had revived it. And the memory of that soft impalpable caress in the darkness of the inn corridor came back to him with a shudder. The girl had first mastered him, and then led him to the one act that was necessary for her purpose. He had been waylaid, after the lapse of centuries—caught, and conquered.

Dimly he realised this, and sought to make plans for his escape. But, for the moment at any rate, he was powerless to manage his thoughts or will, for the sweet, fantastic madness of the whole adventure mounted to his brain like a spell, and he gloried in the feeling that he was utterly enchanted and moving in a world so much larger and wilder than the one he had ever been accustomed to.

The moon, pale and enormous, was just rising over the sea-like plain, when at last he rose to go. Her slanting rays drew all the houses into new perspective, so that their roofs, already glistening with dew, seemed to stretch much higher into the sky than usual, and their gables and quaint old towers lay far away in its purple reaches.

The cathedral appeared unreal in a silver mist. He moved softly, keeping to the shadows; but the streets were all deserted and very silent; the doors were closed, the shutters fastened. Not a soul was astir. The

233

hush of night lay over everything; it was like a town of the dead, a churchyard with gigantic and grotesque tombstones.

Wondering where all the busy life of the day had so utterly disappeared to, he made his way to a back door that entered the inn by means of the stables, thinking thus to reach his room unobserved. He reached the courtyard safely and crossed it by keeping close to the shadow of the wall. He sidled down it, mincing along on tiptoe, just as the old men did when they entered the *salle à manger*. He was horrified to find himself doing this instinctively. A strange impulse came to him, catching him somehow in the centre of his body—an impulse to drop upon all fours and run swiftly and silently. He glanced upwards and the idea came to him to leap up upon his window-sill overhead instead of going round by the stairs. This occurred to him as the easiest, and most natural way. It was like the beginning of some horrible transformation of himself into something else. He was fearfully strung up.

The moon was higher now, and the shadows very dark along the side of the street where he moved. He kept among the deepest of them, and reached the porch with the glass doors.

But here there was light; the inmates, unfortunately, were still about. Hoping to slip across the hall unobserved and reach the stairs, he opened the door carefully and stole in. Then he saw that the hall was not empty. A large dark thing lay against the wall on his left. At first he thought it must be household articles. Then it moved, and he thought it was an immense cat, distorted in some way by the

234

play of light and shadow. Then it rose straight up before him and he saw that it was the proprietress.

What she had been doing in this position he could only venture a dreadful guess, but the moment she stood up and faced him he was aware of some terrible dignity clothing her about that instantly recalled the girl's strange saying that she was a queen. Huge and sinister she stood there under the little oil lamp; alone with him in the empty hall. Awe stirred in his heart, and the roots of some ancient fear. He felt that he must bow to her and make some kind of obeisance. The impulse was fierce and irresistible, as of long habit. He glanced quickly about him. There was no one there. Then he deliberately inclined his head toward her. He bowed.

"Enfin! M'sieur s'est donc décidé. C'est bien alors. J'en suis contente."

Her words came to him sonorously as through a great open space.

Then the great figure came suddenly across the flagged hall at him and seized his trembling hands. Some overpowering force moved with her and caught him.

"On pourrait faire un p'tit tour ensemble, n'est-ce pas? Nous y allons cette nuit et il faut s'exercer un peu d'avance pour cela. Ilsé, Ilsé, viens donc ici. Viens vite!"

And she whirled him round in the opening steps of some dance that seemed oddly and horribly familiar. They made no sound on the stones, this strangely assorted couple. It was all soft and stealthy. And presently, when the air seemed to thicken like smoke, and a red glare as of flame shot through it, he was aware that some one else had joined them and that his hand the mother had released was now tightly held by the daughter. Ilsé had come in answer to the call, and he saw her with leaves of vervain twined in her dark hair, clothed in tattered vestiges of some curious garment, beautiful as the night, and horribly, odiously, loathsomely seductive.

"To the Sabbath! to the Sabbath!" they cried. "On to the Witches' Sabbath!"

Up and down that narrow hall they danced, the women on each side of him, to the wildest measure he had ever imagined, yet which he dimly, dreadfully remembered, till the lamp on the wall flickered and went out, and they were left in total darkness. And the devil woke in his heart with a thousand vile suggestions and made him afraid.

Suddenly they released his hands and he heard the voice of the mother cry that it was time, and they must go. Which way they went he did not pause to see. He only realised that he was free, and he blundered through the darkness till he found the stairs and then tore up them to his room as though all hell was at his heels.

He flung himself on the sofa, with his face in his hands, and groaned. Swiftly reviewing a dozen ways of immediate escape, all equally impossible, he finally decided that the only thing to do for the moment was to sit quiet and wait. He must see what was going to happen. At least in the privacy of his own bedroom he would be fairly safe. The door was locked. He crossed over and softly opened the window which gave upon the courtyard and also permitted a partial view of the hall through the glass doors.

As he did so the hum and murmur of a great activity reached his ears from the streets beyond—the sound of footsteps and voices muffled by distance. He leaned out cautiously and listened. The moonlight was clear and strong now, but his own window was in shadow, the silver disc being still behind the house. It came to him irresistibly that the inhabitants of the town, who a little while before had all been invisible behind closed doors, were now issuing forth, busy upon some secret and unholy errand. He listened intently.

At first everything about him was silent, but soon he became aware of movements going on in the house itself. Rustlings and cheepings came to him across that still, moonlit yard. A concourse of living beings sent the hum of their activity into the night. Things were on the move everywhere. A biting, pungent odour rose through the air, coming he knew not whence. Presently his eyes became glued to the windows of the opposite wall where the moonshine fell in a soft blaze. The roof overhead, and behind him, was reflected clearly in the panes of glass, and he saw the outlines of dark bodies moving with long footsteps over the tiles and along the coping. They passed swiftly and silently, shaped like immense cats, in an endless procession across the pictured glass, and then appeared to leap down to a lower level where he lost sight of them. He just caught the soft thudding of their leaps. Sometimes their shadows fell upon the white wall opposite, and then he could not make out whether they were the shadows of human beings or of cats. They seemed to change swiftly from one to the other. The transformation looked horribly real, for they leaped like human beings, yet changed swiftly in the air immediately afterwards, and dropped like animals.

The yard, too, beneath him, was now alive with the creeping movements of dark forms all stealthily drawing towards the porch with the glass doors. They kept so closely to the wall that he could not determine their actual shape, but when he saw that they passed on to the great congregation that was gathering in the hall, he understood that these were the creatures whose leaping shadows he had first seen reflected in the windowpanes opposite. They were coming from all parts of the town, reaching the appointed meeting-place across the roofs and tiles, and springing from level to level till they came to the yard.

Then a new sound caught his ear, and he saw that the windows all about him were being softly opened, and that to each window came a face. A moment later figures began dropping hurriedly down into the yard. And these figures, as they lowered themselves down from the windows, were human, he saw; but once safely in the yard they fell upon all fours and changed in the swiftest possible second into—cats—huge, silent cats. They ran in streams to join the main body in the hall beyond.

So, after all, the rooms in the house had not been empty and unoccupied.

Moreover, what he saw no longer filled him with amazement. For he remembered it all. It was familiar. It had all happened before just so, hundreds of times, and he himself had taken part in it and known the wild madness of it all. The outline of the old building changed, the yard grew larger, and he seemed to be staring down upon it from a much greater height through smoky vapours. And, as he looked, half remembering, the old pains of long ago, fierce and sweet, furiously assailed him, and the blood stirred horribly as he heard the Call of the Dance again in his heart and tasted the ancient magic of Ilsé whirling by his side.

Suddenly he started back. A great lithe cat had leaped softly up from the shadows below on to the sill close to his face, and was staring fixedly at him with the eyes of a human. "Come," it seemed to say, "come with us to the Dance! Change as of old! Transform yourself swiftly and come!" Only too well he understood the creature's soundless call.

It was gone again in a flash with scarcely a sound of its padded feet on the stones, and then others dropped by the score down the side of the house, past his very eyes, all changing as they fell and darting away rapidly, softly, towards the gathering point. And again he felt the dreadful desire to do likewise; to murmur the old incantation, and then drop upon hands and knees and run swiftly for the great flying leap into the air. Oh, how the passion of it rose within him like a flood, twisting his very entrails, sending his heart's desire flaming forth into the night for the old, old Dance of the Sorcerers at the Witches' Sabbath! The whirl of the stars was about him; once more he met the magic of the moon. The power of the wind, rushing from precipice and forest, leaping from cliff to cliff across the valleys, tore him away.... He heard the cries of the dancers and their wild laughter, and with this savage girl in his embrace he danced furiously about the dim Throne where sat the Figure with the sceptre of majesty....

Then, suddenly, all became hushed and still, and the fever died down a little in his heart. The calm moonlight flooded a courtyard empty and deserted. They had started. The procession was off into the sky. And he was left behind—alone.

Vezin tiptoed softly across the room and unlocked the door. The murmur from the streets, growing momentarily as he advanced, met his ears. He made his way with the utmost caution down the corridor. At the head of the stairs he paused and listened. Below him, the hall where they had gathered was dark and still, but through opened doors and windows on the far side of the building came the sound of a great throng moving farther and farther into the distance.

He made his way down the creaking wooden stairs, dreading yet longing to meet some straggler who should point the way, but finding no one; across the dark hall, so lately thronged with living, moving things, and out through the opened front doors into the street. He could not believe that he was really left behind, really forgotten, that he had been purposely permitted to escape. It perplexed him.

Nervously he peered about him, and up and down the street; then, seeing nothing, advanced slowly down the pavement.

The whole town, as he went, showed itself empty and deserted, as though a great wind had blown everything alive out of it. The doors and windows of the houses stood open to the night; nothing stirred;

moonlight and silence lay over all. The night lay about him like a cloak. The air, soft and cool, caressed his cheek like the touch of a great furry paw. He gained confidence and began to walk quickly, though still keeping to the shadowed side. Nowhere could he discover the faintest sign of the great unholy exodus he knew had just taken place. The moon sailed high over all in a sky cloudless and serene.

Hardly realising where he was going, he crossed the open market-place and so came to the ramparts, whence he knew a pathway descended to the high road and along which he could make good his escape to one of the other little towns that lay to the northward, and so to the railway.

But first he paused and gazed out over the scene at his feet where the great plain lay like a silver map of some dream country. The still beauty of it entered his heart, increasing his sense of bewilderment and unreality. No air stirred, the leaves of the plane trees stood motionless, the near details were defined with the sharpness of day against dark shadows, and in the distance the fields and woods melted away into haze and shimmering mistiness.

But the breath caught in his throat and he stood stockstill as though transfixed when his gaze passed from the horizon and fell upon the near prospect in the depth of the valley at his feet. The whole lower slopes of the hill, that lay hid from the brightness of the moon, were aglow, and through the glare he saw countless moving forms, shifting thick and fast between the openings of the trees; while overhead, like leaves driven by the wind, he discerned flying shapes that hovered darkly one moment against the sky and then settled down with cries and weird singing through the branches into the region that was aflame.

Spellbound, he stood and stared for a time that he could not measure. And then, moved by one of the terrible impulses that seemed to control the whole adventure, he climbed swiftly upon the top of the broad coping, and balanced a moment where the valley gaped at his feet. But in that very instant, as he stood hovering, a sudden movement among the shadows of the houses caught his eye, and he turned to see the outline of a large animal dart swiftly across the open space behind him, and land with a flying leap upon the top of the wall a little lower down. It ran like the wind to his feet and then rose up beside him upon the ramparts. A shiver seemed to run through the moonlight, and his sight trembled for a second. His heart pulsed fearfully. Ilsé stood beside him, peering into his face.

Some dark substance, he saw, stained the girl's face and skin, shining in the moonlight as she stretched her hands towards him; she was dressed in wretched tattered garments that yet became her mightily; rue and vervain twined about her temples; her eyes glittered with unholy light. He only just controlled the wild impulse to take her in his arms and leap with her from their giddy perch into the valley below.

"See!" she cried, pointing with an arm on which the rags fluttered in the rising wind towards the forest aglow in the distance. "See where they await us! The woods are alive! Already the Great Ones are there, and the dance will soon begin! The salve is here! Anoint yourself and come!"

Though a moment before the sky was clear and cloudless, yet even while she spoke the face of the moon grew dark and the wind began to toss in the crests of the plane trees at his feet. Stray gusts brought the sounds of hoarse singing and crying from the lower slopes of the hill, and the pungent odour he had already noticed about the courtyard of the inn rose about him in the air.

"Transform, transform!" she cried again, her voice rising like a song. "Rub well your skin before you fly. Come! Come with me to the Sabbath, to the madness of its furious delight, to the sweet abandonment of its evil worship! See! the Great Ones are there, and the terrible Sacraments prepared. The Throne is occupied. Anoint and come! Anoint and come!"

She grew to the height of a tree beside him, leaping upon the wall with flaming eyes and hair strewn upon the night. He too began to change swiftly. Her hands touched the skin of his face and neck, streaking him with the burning salve that sent the old magic into his blood with the power before which fades all that is good.

A wild roar came up to his ears from the heart of the wood, and the girl, when she heard it, leaped upon the wall in the frenzy of her wicked joy.

"Satan is there!" she screamed, rushing upon him and striving to draw him with her to the edge of the wall. "Satan has come. The Sacraments call us! Come, with your dear apostate soul, and we will

243

worship and dance till the moon dies and the world is forgotten!"

Just saving himself from the dreadful plunge, Vezin struggled to release himself from her grasp, while the passion tore at his reins and all but mastered him. He shrieked aloud, not knowing what he said, and then he shrieked again. It was the old impulses, the old awful habits instinctively finding voice; for though it seemed to him that he merely shrieked nonsense, the words he uttered really had meaning in them, and were intelligible. It was the ancient call. And it was heard below. It was answered.

The wind whistled at the skirts of his coat as the air round him darkened with many flying forms crowding upwards out of the valley. The crying of hoarse voices smote upon his ears, coming closer. Strokes of wind buffeted him, tearing him this way and that along the crumbling top of the stone wall; and Ilsé clung to him with her long shining arms, smooth and bare, holding him fast about the neck. But not Ilsé alone, for a dozen of them surrounded him, dropping out of the air. The pungent odour of the anointed bodies stifled him, exciting him to the old madness of the Sabbath, the dance of the witches and sorcerers doing honour to the personified Evil of the world.

"Anoint and away! Anoint and away!" they cried in wild chorus about him. "To the Dance that never dies! To the sweet and fearful fantasy of evil!"

Another moment and he would have yielded and gone, for his will turned soft and the flood of passionate memory all but overwhelmed him, when— so can a small thing after the whole course of an

244

adventure—he caught his foot upon a loose stone in the edge of the wall, and then fell with a sudden crash on to the ground below. But he fell towards the houses, in the open space of dust and cobblestones, and fortunately not into the gaping depth of the valley on the farther side.

And they, too, came in a tumbling heap about him, like flies upon a piece of food, but as they fell he was released for a moment from the power of their touch, and in that brief instant of freedom there flashed into his mind the sudden intuition that saved him. Before he could regain his feet he saw them scrabbling awkwardly back upon the wall, as though bat-like they could only fly by dropping from a height, and had no hold upon him in the open. Then, seeing them perched there in a row like cats upon a roof, all dark and singularly shapeless, their eyes like lamps, the sudden memory came back to him of Ilsé's terror at the sight of fire.

Quick as a flash he found his matches and lit the dead leaves that lay under the wall.

Dry and withered, they caught fire at once, and the wind carried the flame in a long line down the length of the wall, licking upwards as it ran; and with shrieks and wailings, the crowded row of forms upon the top melted away into the air on the other side, and were gone with a great rush and whirring of their bodies down into the heart of the haunted valley, leaving Vezin breathless and shaken in the middle of the deserted ground.

"Ilsé!" he called feebly; "Ilsé!" for his heart ached to think that she was really gone to the great Dance without him, and that he had lost the opportunity of its fearful joy. Yet at the same time his relief was so great, and he was so dazed and troubled in mind with the whole thing, that he hardly knew what he was saying, and only cried aloud in the fierce storm of his emotion....

The fire under the wall ran its course, and the moonlight came out again, soft and clear, from its temporary eclipse. With one last shuddering look at the ruined ramparts, and a feeling of horrid wonder for the haunted valley beyond, where the shapes still crowded and flew, he turned his face towards the town and slowly made his way in the direction of the hotel.

And as he went, a great wailing of cries, and a sound of howling, followed him from the gleaming forest below, growing fainter and fainter with the bursts of wind as he disappeared between the houses.

VI

"It may seem rather abrupt to you, this sudden tame ending," said Arthur Vezin, glancing with flushed face and timid eyes at Dr. Silence sitting there with his notebook, "but the fact is—er—from that moment my memory seems to have failed rather. I have no distinct recollection of how I got home or what precisely I did.

"It appears I never went back to the inn at all. I only dimly recollect racing down a long white road in the moonlight, past woods and villages, still and deserted, and then the dawn came up, and I saw the towers of a biggish town and so came to a station.

"But, long before that, I remember pausing somewhere on the road and looking back to where the hill-town of my adventure stood up in the moonlight, and thinking how exactly like a great monstrous cat it lay there upon the plain, its huge front paws lying down the two main streets, and the twin and broken towers of the cathedral marking its torn ears against the sky. That picture stays in my mind with the utmost vividness to this day.

"Another thing remains in my mind from that escape—namely, the sudden sharp reminder that I had not paid my bill, and the decision I made, standing there on the dusty highroad, that the small baggage I had left behind would more than settle for my indebtedness.

"For the rest, I can only tell you that I got coffee and bread at a café on the outskirts of this town I had come to, and soon after found my way to the station and caught a train later in the day. That same evening I reached London."

"And how long altogether," asked John Silence quietly, "do you think you stayed in the town of the adventure?"

Vezin looked up sheepishly.

"I was coming to that," he resumed, with apologetic wrigglings of his body. "In London I found that I was a whole week out in my reckoning of time. I had stayed over a week in the town, and it ought to have been September 15th,—instead of which it was only September 10th!"

"So that, in reality, you had only stayed a night or two in the inn?" queried the doctor.

Vezin hesitated before replying. He shuffled upon the mat.

"I must have gained time somewhere," he said at length—"somewhere or somehow. I certainly had a week to my credit. I can't explain it. I can only give you the fact."

"And this happened to you last year, since when you have never been back to the place?"

"Last autumn, yes," murmured Vezin; "and I have never dared to go back. I think I never want to."

"And, tell me," asked Dr. Silence at length, when he saw that the little man had evidently come to the end of his words and had nothing more to say, "had you ever read up the subject of the old witchcraft practices during the Middle Ages, or been at all interested in the subject?"

"Never!" declared Vezin emphatically. "I had never given a thought to such matters so far as I know—"

"Or to the question of reincarnation, perhaps?"

"Never—before my adventure; but I have since," he replied significantly.

There was, however, something still on the man's mind that he wished to relieve himself of by confession, yet could only with difficulty bring himself to mention; and it was only after the sympathetic tactfulness of the doctor had provided numerous openings that he at length availed himself of one of them, and stammered that he would like to show him the marks he still had on his neck where, he said, the girl had touched him with her anointed hands.

He took off his collar after infinite fumbling hesitation, and lowered his shirt a little for the doctor to see. And there, on the surface of the skin, lay a faint reddish line across the shoulder and extending a little way down the back towards the spine. It certainly indicated exactly the position an arm might have taken in the act of embracing. And on the other side of the neck, slightly higher up, was a similar mark, though not quite so clearly defined.

"That was where she held me that night on the ramparts," he whispered, a strange light coming and going in his eyes.

It was some weeks later when I again found occasion to consult John Silence concerning another extraordinary case that had come under my notice, and we fell to discussing Vezin's story. Since hearing it, the doctor had made investigations on his own account, and one of his secretaries had discovered that Vezin's ancestors had actually lived for generations in the very town where the adventure came to him. Two of them, both women, had been tried and convicted as witches, and had been burned alive at the stake. Moreover, it had not been difficult to prove that the very inn where Vezin stayed was built about 1700 upon the spot where the funeral pyres stood and the executions took place. The town was a sort of headquarters for all the sorcerers and witches of the entire region, and after conviction they were burnt there literally by scores.

"It seems strange," continued the doctor, "that Vezin should have remained ignorant of all this; but, on the other hand, it was not the kind of history that successive generations would have been anxious to keep alive, or to repeat to their children. Therefore I am inclined to think he still knows nothing about it.

"The whole adventure seems to have been a very vivid revival of the memories of an earlier life, caused by coming directly into contact with the living forces still intense enough to hang about the place, and, by a most singular chance, too, with the very souls who had taken part with him in the events of that particular life. For the mother and daughter who impressed him so strangely must have been leading actors, with himself, in the scenes and practices of witchcraft which at that period dominated the imaginations of the whole country.

"One has only to read the histories of the times to know that these witches claimed the power of transforming themselves into various animals, both for the purposes of disguise and also to convey themselves swiftly to the scenes of their imaginary orgies. Lycanthropy, or the power to change themselves into wolves, was everywhere believed in, and the ability to transform themselves into cats by rubbing their bodies with a special salve or ointment provided by Satan himself, found equal credence. The witchcraft trials abound in evidences of such universal beliefs."

Dr. Silence quoted chapter and verse from many writers on the subject, and showed how every detail of Vezin's adventure had a basis in the practices of those dark days.

"But that the entire affair took place subjectively in the man's own consciousness, I have no doubt," he went on, in reply to my questions; "for my secretary who has been to the town to investigate, discovered his signature in the visitors' book, and proved by it that he had arrived on September 8th, and left suddenly without paying his bill. He left two days later, and they still were in possession of his dirty brown bag and some tourist clothes. I paid a few francs in settlement of his debt, and have sent his luggage on to him. The daughter was absent from home, but the proprietress, a large woman very much as he described her, told my secretary that he had seemed a very strange, absent-minded kind of gentleman, and after his disappearance she had feared for a long time that he had met with a violent end in the neighbouring forest where he used to roam about alone.

"I should like to have obtained a personal interview with the daughter so as to ascertain how much was subjective and how much actually took place with her as Vezin told it. For her dread of fire and the sight of burning must, of course, have been the intuitive memory of her former painful death at the stake, and have thus explained why he fancied more than once that he saw her through smoke and flame."

"And that mark on his skin, for instance?" I inquired.

"Merely the marks produced by hysterical brooding," he replied, "like the stigmata of the *religieuses*, and the bruises which appear on the bodies of hypnotised subjects who have been told to expect them. This is very common and easily explained. Only it seems curious that these marks should have remained so long in Vezin's case. Usually they disappear quickly."

"Obviously he is still thinking about it all, brooding, and living it all over again," I ventured.

"Probably. And this makes me fear that the end of his trouble is not yet. We shall hear of him again. It is a case, alas! I can do little to alleviate."

Dr. Silence spoke gravely and with sadness in his voice.

"And what do you make of the Frenchman in the train?" I asked further—"the man who warned him against the place, *à cause du sommeil et à cause des chats?* Surely a very singular incident?"

"A very singular incident indeed," he made answer slowly, "and one I can only explain on the basis of a highly improbable coincidence—"

"Namely?"

"That the man was one who had himself stayed in the town and undergone there a similar experience. I should like to find this man and ask him. But the crystal is useless here, for I have no slightest clue to go upon, and I can only conclude that some singular psychic affinity, some force still active in his being out of the same past life, drew him thus to the personality of Vezin, and enabled him to fear what might happen to him, and thus to warn him as he did.

"Yes," he presently continued, half talking to himself, "I suspect in this case that Vezin was swept into the vortex of forces arising out of the intense activities of a past life, and that he lived over again a scene in which he had often played a leading part centuries before. For strong actions set up forces that are so slow to exhaust themselves, they may be said in a sense never to die. In this case they were not vital enough to render the illusion complete, so that the little man found himself caught in a very distressing confusion of the present and the past; yet he was sufficiently sensitive to recognise that it was true, and to fight against the degradation of returning, even in memory, to a former and lower state of development.

"Ah yes!" he continued, crossing the floor to gaze at the darkening sky, and seemingly quite oblivious of my presence, "subliminal up-rushes of memory like this can be exceedingly painful, and sometimes exceedingly dangerous. I only trust that this gentle soul may soon escape from this obsession of a passionate and tempestuous past. But I doubt it, I doubt it."

His voice was hushed with sadness as he spoke, and when he turned back into the room again there was an expression of profound yearning upon his face, the yearning of a soul whose desire to help is sometimes greater than his power.

About the Ascension Epoch

Ascension Epoch is a shared universe for original fiction. It was originally created by Mike and Shell DiBaggio as a setting for their superhero and adventure stories, built around an alternate history that incorporates many details from public domain literature, movies, and comic books. All of the stories, characters, and artwork are open source, licensed under a Creative Commons Attribution-ShareAlike license, meaning anyone is free to reshare or create derivative works, even for profit, as long as they credit the original creators and link back to our site. The setting was built to encourage collaboration with other writers and artists. To learn more, please visit our website http://www.ascensionepoch.cc

Enjoy the Book? Let us Know!

Few things make Mike and Shell happier than hearing from people who enjoyed their work. Feel free to contact them on the web at ascensionepoch.com or by email at mike@ ascensionepoch.com or shellpresto@ ascensionepoch.com.

If you really want to make their day, then leave a review wherever you purchased this book, and then tell all your friends about us! You can 'Like' our Facebook page, circle us on Google Plus, and talk us up on Twitter with the #AscensionEpoch tag.

Other Ascension Epoch Stories

Copper Knights and Granite Men

COPPER KNIGHTS AND GRANITE MEN

MICHAEL A. DIBAGGIO
SHELL 'PRESTO' DIBAGGIO

A pretentious super-powered musician; his ageless, techno-wizard adoptive father; and an ex-army officer with radioactive organs walk into a museum — and find everyone turned to stone! But this is no joke! It's a sinister threat that only the Challenger Foundation, the World's Greatest Adventurers, can handle.

A witty and suspenseful superhero adventure that draws from the King in Yellow mythos and taps the secret occult history of North America, Copper Knights and Granite Men is the first book in the Challenger Confidential series.

256

Population of Loss

The Martian onslaught has crushed earth's mightiest empires and reduced the great achievements of civilization to poisoned rubble, but mankind still endures.

From the ruins of England to the desolate American west, unexpected champions arise to confront a foe that has never yet known defeat, and the stakes are nothing less than the survival of the human race.

Population of Loss, the first volume in the Martian War Chronicles, contains four short stories of superheroes and paranormal menace set amid the carnage of the War of the Worlds.

House of Refuge

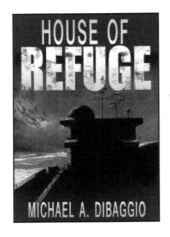

Justin Agnarsson is stationkeeper and lone crewman of South Atlantic House of Refuge #49, a floating sanctuary for the thousands of mariners and seasteading families who live and work in the 350-mile long Plata Raft. Now, war threatens to bring an end to his lifesaving mission as an Argentine warship pursues a pair of refugees to the station. A house of refuge is supposed to be inviolable, but the Argentines are hell bent on their mission. Alone and virtually defenseless, Agnarsson faces an impossible choice between duty and survival. But when the brutality of war threatens to unravel the fabric of civilization, more than lives are at stake.

Second place winner of the 2014 Libertarian Fiction Authors/Students for Liberty Short Fiction Contest

About the Creators

Mike and Shell are a husband and wife team whose love for storytelling began with an early passion for superhero comics, SF/Fantasy novels, and role playing games. When they're not writing or illustrating, they can often be found hiking, building Legos, customizing action figures, or watching old horror movies. They live in St. Clair, Pennsylvania, along with their three dogs and two cats.